One ok

Keith R. Rees

Savant Books and Publications
Honolulu, HI, USA
2018

Published in the USA by Savant Books and Publications
2630 Kapiolani Blvd #1601
Honolulu, HI 96826
http://www.savantbooksandpublications.com

Printed in the USA

Edited by Helen R. Davis
Cover Design by Daniel S. Janik
Cover Images (with permission)
  Night | laocaohenmang - Pixabay (CC0 creative commons)
  Eyes of God | Spirit111 - Pixabay (CC0 creative commons)
  Chess | ERICW - Pixabay (CC0 creative commons)

Copyright 2017 Keith Rees. All rights reserved. No part of this work may be reproduced without the prior written permission of the author.

13 digit ISBN: 9780997247299

All names, characters, places and incidents are fictitious or used fictitiously. Any resemblance to actual persons, living or dead, and any places or events is purely coincidental.

First Edition: June 2018
Library of Congress Control Number: 2018906454

Dedication

For my daughter, Isabella

Acknowledgements

Kindness Be Conceived – Written by Thao Nguyen and featuring Joanna Newsom – Copyright 2013; From the album, We the Common

A Passage to Bangkok – Lyrics by Neal Peart – Copyright 1976; From the album, Rush 2112

Segment with the story of the Bald Eagle – An homage to the 1992 Geoff Murphy film, Freejack

Prologue

A dazzling and luminous sphere slowly bounded over the wooden cracks of the rickety floor. It sparkled and shimmered with brilliant golds and flashes of silver as it rolled and bounced in slow motion. The ball was transparent with wondrous colors of gold, silver and black trapped within the heart of the orb. Within the ribbons different shades of blacks, reds and silvers, interlaced and with each tiny tap on the floor the colors glittered with other-worldly brilliance. With each bounce, the round object became larger and larger until it nearly overwhelmed its target. As it appeared as if it were about to roll right over the top of one's self...

He startled awake. Miles Devereaux lifted his head and gasped for air. He had been asleep at a table, his head resting on his folded arms. He looked around in a panic. At first, he did not know where he was. It was still dark outside, but the wind seemed to be howling all around the shadowy windows. He looked around the place where he was but it was empty. He sat alone at a booth next to a window. A gust of wind slapped beads of rain against the pane, causing Miles to flinch his head for fear of getting wet, too. Then as he quickly gathered his thoughts, Miles realized where he was. He had fallen asleep at one of his usual hangouts: Reggie's Tavern.

Miles rubbed his eyes and placed the palms of his hands against his forehead. "Oh *man*," he groaned out loud. "Oh, my head. Boy, did I sleep."

He looked around the tavern searching for the wall clock. He knew there was one behind the bar. He spotted the red digital numbers in the dimly lit pub. It was a few minutes past five in the morning. On seeing the time, Miles became more alert and even a bit frightened. *Why am I here so early in the morning? And what is causing so much commotion outside?* His mind began to race, trying to remember what had happened the night before. He stared at the table, trying to shake the cobwebs loose in his mind. He glanced over at the salt and pepper shakers sitting on the end of the table against the wall. They sat right next to a napkin dispenser with a couple of faded menus standing sideways between the napkins and the wall. The faded yellow letters of the tavern's logo curved downward. It was then, staring at the old menu, that something clicked in his mind. He froze in his seat, the wind howling outside. "Vicky, Viv and Cas…" he whispered to himself.

Just then a door flung open behind the bar and large black

man came striding in with a white towel draped over his shoulder. Keys rattled from his fingers as he quickly made his way towards the front entrance of the tavern. As he crossed the floor, his sneakers skidded to a halt. With his eyes wide in disbelief, the big man bellowed, "Miles? What the hell you still doin' here, man?"

Miles sat up straight in the booth. He did not quite know what to say. He did not even know why he was there, or how he had gotten there in the first place. He opened his mouth, but all that came out was, "Reggie?"

Reggie hurried over to the table and grabbed Miles' arm. He urged him to get up. "Hey man, we got's to go. What you still doin' here? I coulda sworn you left not long ago with everybody else."

Miles coughed a bit as he tried to stand. "Huh?" he gasped between coughs. His legs felt like they were weighted down with cement. He was so tired he could barely move. "I... I guess I fell asleep."

Reggie shook his head. Noticing the strange clothing Miles was wearing, Reggie commented, "Damn Miles, what kind of look you goin' for, man? Them clothes look like you stole 'em off a hobo." Reggie let out a big laugh at his own joke. Miles glanced down at his odd clothing, but it confused him even further so he said nothing.

Reggie could not believe anybody was still in his tavern,

especially with this kind of storm coming. "It's some serious stuff goin' on out there, man. You need to get home and get low." He unlocked the front door and peered out into the raging night. Raising his voice over the rain, he said, "You gonna be okay goin' back to yo buildin' in this?" The two men glanced down at the umbrella bucket that stood just inside the entrance but it was empty. "I'd give ya one of those if I had one, but I don't think it'd do ya much good in this mess."

"That's alright," Miles answered. All of a sudden, he was extremely eager to get home. Not because of the torrential rain, but for totally different reasons; reasons that began to flood from memory almost as fast as it was raining outside. "You okay getting home, Reggie?"

"Yeah, don't worry 'bout me, man. I'm just around the corner. You just get yo ass home."

"Alright!" Miles shouted over the melee. "See you on the other side, man."

With that, Miles dashed out into the fury.

The rain pelted Miles in the face and battered his old worn out clothes. He had no idea where he got such clothes or why he had them on now. The rain soaked right through them and clung to his narrow frame. They felt like weights on his shoulders.

He jogged down the darkened streets in the rain. He noticed that it was not really raining that hard. It was a lighter rain than the torrent he had heard back at the tavern. No, it was the *wind* that took him by surprise. The wind seemed to swirl and even knock him off his feet as he jogged. He could not believe how tough it was to simply jog in it. He could not run any faster than a slow jog because he was so tired. He soon realized that the weight of his clothing was mostly due to the heavy jacket he was wearing. *Why am I wearing a coat?* Miles wondered to himself. *It's late summer here and not cold at all.* As he jogged he tried his best to pull the wet, soggy coat off his arms. He screamed and cursed at it as he struggled to pull the messy heap off his body. "Get off me, damnit." A sleeve tore. He pulled harder as he stumbled down another darkened alley. Finally, he freed himself from the water-logged old coat and tossed it angrily to the ground and kept running.

"Yeah, that's much better," he murmured to himself.

He felt around in his pockets as he ran in hopes of finding his cell phone. He was increasingly worried about his wife and two kids at home.

Vivian was the oldest, a spry young lady of five years who was already an 'expert at everything,' as she put it delicately in her own words. Even when she helped her mother in the kitchen mixing a batch of cookies, Vivian would always say something like, "I'm an expert mixer!" Or if she was studying her spelling words for school, she would say, "I'm an expert speller. Ask me anything," as she would broadly smile at her parents.

Casden was the youngest. He had just turned one a few months earlier in the summer and had finally begun to master walking on his own. He had chubby cheeks with a single, yet very darkened, freckle on his right cheek. Just like any young toddler, he got into everything as he was curious about everything.

One of Vivian's favorite things to do with her dad was to challenge him to a game of chess. Miles loved to play and had learned from his father at a young age just as Vivian was learning. Even for a five-year old going on fifteen, she had a clear understanding of the game and knew what moves every single piece could and could not make. Her favorite pieces were the bishops because they could 'shoot clear across the board,' as she would put it, and 'take anyone down.' Even Casden, or Cas as he was known, would watch intently as they played. He could not wait for pieces to be discarded, then he knew he could grab them and play with them.

Miles desperately felt around his soaking pockets but could not find his phone anywhere. *It wouldn't do much good in this mess anyway,* he thought to himself. His main concern was his wife, Victoria. She was two and a half months pregnant and just had begun to show a small bump on her tummy. They had only found out a few weeks earlier that she was pregnant with their third child. The next morning they had decided to share the good news with their friends.

Even though she was still in her first trimester, he was quite concerned about her. She had had a rough pregnancy with Cas and spent most of her time in bed the remaining three weeks before he was born. It was then that Vivian had to do some quick growing as she helped her dad around the house while her mom was laid up in bed. It was a rough time for all of them, but they made it through and had become a much closer family as a result.

As his memory slowly came back to him, he began to realize what was going on. *The hurricane,* he thought to himself. *It's hitting right now.* The storm was much worse than Miles had ever imagined it would be. He shook his head at his carelessness. He knew they should have evacuated a day or two before, but they had both agreed that they could ride it out, thinking the storm would hit much further east from them.

He had several more blocks to go before he would reach their apartment building. He could spot their building easily as it was the only one that had reddish and white bricks that lined the edges of the roof. It stood out amongst the rows of apartment buildings that lined the old streets. The rest of the buildings had plain brown or black faded bricks on them that gave them an aged and rundown look.

He wondered again how he ended up at Reggie's alone and dressed so strangely. *Where had I been?* his mind raced.

What happened to me? How did I get there? Flashes of memories began flooding his mind again. He remembered seeing cities: ancient ones, destroyed ones, and even modern, space-age metropolises that seemed to extend as far as the eye could see, shimmering and glowing brilliantly in the night sky. Then he saw cities in total ruin, in piles of rubble. He did not understand what they were or how he had such memories. Then he saw a flash of sunshine: a tropical setting. There were palm trees swaying in the air.

Suddenly, a gust of wind blew him sideways and into a couple of metal garbage cans. He caught himself on a rain-soaked railing that led to one of the many apartment buildings. "Damn, that wind is something else. Geez!" he shouted. It was then, in the darkness and through the sideways rain, he saw the familiar reddish and white bricks near the edge of the roof of a building one block up.

"Vicky!" he yelled out. Their apartment was on the top floor of the four-story building. He knew the elevator would be out in this kind of weather, so he would have to race up the stairs.

A strong sensation began to well up inside Miles. He suddenly realized why he was in such a rush to get back upstairs. As he reached the railing of the steps to his building's front door, he instantly remembered it seemed he had stood here before. In this same exact way and in a terrible storm just like this one. Not only did it seem like he had been in this position before, he *had* been in this position before, "Oh, my God," he whimpered, "not again…" Grabbing the railing, he lunged up the steps and slipped on the first one. As he grabbed the doorknob, he shouted in distress, "It can't happen again! Vicky!"

He dashed across the lobby and slammed into the wall next to the door to the stairwell. He flung the door open. "Vicky! Cas! Vivian!" he shouted up the stairwell. "No, no, no…" He leaped up the stairs, two, three, at a time. His panic and distress grew with each leap upward.

The dream he had just before waking at Reggie's began playing itself over and over in his mind as he climbed each step. The glassy, transparent orb bounced in slow motion down the old floor of his apartment hallway, glittering with gold and silvery light. Each tap on the floor sounded like a crash of thunder. The sound boomed inside Miles' head like a pounding drum. "No!" he shouted over and over, "let it go!" He reached the third floor and flew up the final flight as quickly as he could in sheer panic. "Cas! Don't do it! Stop!"

Inside apartment 405, young Cas sat at the end of the hallway playing with a small sack of marbles. There were five in all, each decorated with fancy bright colors that made him smile in delight. All of them had single colors except for one. One marble stood out from all the rest. Inside it were bands of gold, silver, and black mixed with red, with shiny pieces of glitter outlining the bands. He tossed them one at a time and laughed as each one rolled down the hallway towards the front door.

"Cas," a familiar voice called out from one of the bedrooms. "Stop throwing those things. This is your last warning, buddy."

His father peeked his head around the corner and stared at him. "I told you, no more, Son. It's too noisy and we need to get ready to go." With that, Cas tossed the last marble down the hallway.

With each bounce, the marble flashed with glittery light and Cas watched in awe and amazement as the wondrous marble tapped across the floor.

"I said no, Cas," Miles blurted out. He lunged after the marble to try and keep it from knocking loudly against the walls and the door.

Just as he was lunging to catch the marble, the front door flew open. A wet and soggy Miles slid to the floor in a heap of desperation. "No!" he shouted. But that was the only thing that could escape his mouth. In a flash of terror, he watched helplessly as the other Miles sprang forward with his outstretched hand to catch the dazzling marble. The second the marble touched his hand, it glowed an amazing sky blue, and the other Miles disappeared into thin air.

Chapter 1
The Terminal

Miles took his seat on the airplane as it came in for a landing. He sat near the window and watched as the plane glided in slowly. It was nighttime, or maybe early evening. He was not quite sure what time it was. In fact, he was not quite sure where he was even flying to. He could not remember.

He had just awakened from what seemed like several hours of sleep. He stretched his toes in his shoes and tried his best to stretch his arms without disturbing the person sitting next to him. As he tried to shake the sleep from his eyes, he slowly noticed his surroundings. The seats in front of him were much further away than normal. He tried to remember if he had been moved up to first class or business class, but he could not. *Lots of leg room*, he thought to himself. *Very nice!* Glancing over at his seat companion, he could tell that the enormous man was happy about the ample leg room as well. He was a tremendous man with dark skin and stared straight ahead as if he were in a trance. Miles straightened in his seat and tried not to stare at him. *I'd hate to tick this guy off*, he thought to himself. He gazed around the cabin but no one was standing and he did not see any flight attendants. He could tell the plane was descending so he assumed they would be landing shortly. What he did notice was the unusual cabin of the aircraft. The length and the width were abundantly large. Larger than any plane he had ever been on before. *Wow!* he thought. *This must be one of those fancy new ones.*

Then, he glanced outside the cabin window and did a double-take. With an astonished look on his face, he swirled in his seat and planted both hands and his face on the glass. "Whoa," he exclaimed. He glanced over at the large man next to him, but he did not even acknowledge Miles' excitement. Miles stared out his window in amazement. The city below was enormous. He knew they were still very high in the air, but he had never seen a city from the air at night with such sheer size. The twinkling lights glowed all the way over the horizon and beyond. "Holy cow. Where *are* we?" he blurted out again. This question did produce a slight head turn from his seatmate. The look on his face implied that it was obvious. How could anyone not know where they were flying?

Miles was glued to his window. As the airplane slowly descended, he could begin to make out more details of the city below. There appeared to be high rises and skyscrapers everywhere. Not just average concrete buildings; these were metallic and glass-mirrored buildings that all shimmered in the night sky. They were sleek in design and ranged in all manner of shapes and sizes. The impressive sight stretched as far as the eye could see. It was the most modern and futuristic city he had ever laid eyes on.

Then he noticed the network of highways and roads that lined the city. They were all lit up brilliantly as they flew over. He looked more curiously as he saw that the vehicles on the roads were not moving slowly as they normally would appear from a great height. No, not in this city. These cars zipped across the highways fluidly like blips in a video game or a cartoon. Miles shook his head. *What is this place?* his mind scrambled. He had had enough. He finally tapped the enormous man next to him on the shoulder. He did not care if the man became irritated. With the expression on the big man's face, that seemed quite possible, but Miles did not care. "Hey, buddy. I ain't no Albert Einstein, but is it me or are those cars down there really haulin' ass?" The man just tilted his head and grimaced even more, ignoring Miles' question.

Miles shook his head when he received no answer. He went back to examining the incredible city below as the plane came in for a landing. He stared in awe as he began to make out the shiny transports more clearly as they zipped along the roads in all directions. They did not look like regular cars and trucks; they resembled something more like the modern train cars of the bullet trains used in Europe or Asia. Each individual vehicle was a rounded, glass-incased tube that seemed to glide effortlessly and at great speeds across the city. "This is incredible," he said out loud again. "Unbelievable."

Soon, the plane began to slow down to what seemed to be an almost taxiing speed. Suddenly the windows were blackened over and he could no longer see the city below. From one moment to the next, the dazzling display of light outside suddenly turned to dark. "What the..." But before Miles could tell that they had landed, the aircraft came to a stop. He sat up tensely in his chair and folded his arms. He looked around the cabin but no one was moving; everyone remained in their seats. Every window in the cabin was darkened. Soon, additional cabin lights began to flicker above the seating area.

"Wow, this is some airplane. I didn't even feel the landing," Miles said under his breath. "Smoothest landing I've ever had, that's for damn sure."

A voice came over the loudspeakers in the cabin. The female voice spoke in a language that Miles did not understand. He tried his best to remember why he was on this trip. He began to feel worried and a little frightened as well. *Why can't I remember where I was going?* he asked himself over and over in his mind. Suddenly, bit by bit, memories began to creep back into his consciousness. He remembered the storm, the swirling rain. He remembered the overwhelming panic and urge to flee. "Whoa, whoa, *whoa*. Wait a minute," he whispered to himself. "*Vicky*."

After the voice on the intercom stopped speaking in the unfamiliar language, the same voice began speaking in English. "Ladies and gentlemen, the aircraft has landed. Please remain seated until the captain has turned off the seatbelt indicator. Disembarkation will begin shortly. The current temperature is twenty-two degrees."

"Ah crap," Miles moaned.

"The local time is 9:02 P.M." Miles looked at his watch. He quickly removed it and began to set the current time, but he noticed his analog watch was already set to the correct time. "We thank you for flying with us and hope you enjoyed your journey. Mind the overhead compartments and be courteous to your fellow passengers when disembarking. Please enjoy your stay. Welcome to Bangkok."

Miles' jaw dropped. At the very least, he was expecting a large city in California, or perhaps Canada. But not the Far East. The seatbelt indicator was turned off and people began to stand and grab their belongings from the overhead bins. "Did she just say 'Bangkok'?" Miles asked to anyone who was listening. No one was. Everyone either ignored him, or thought he was crazy for not knowing where he was flying to. Miles glanced at the overhead bin but he did not see any luggage that looked familiar. It appeared he did not have any carry-on baggage at all. What troubled him the most was why he had traveled so far in the first place. It did not make sense to him at all. "Thailand?" he bellowed once again.

"Yes, Thailand!" a cheerful voice said behind him. He whirled around to see who it was. It was one of the flight attendants standing in the middle of all the passengers in the aisle. She was only a few rows back.

"Oh. You speak English?" Miles asked hopefully.

"Yes, Thailand," she said again happily. "Welcome, welcome."

The line did not seem to be moving to get off the plane. Everyone just stood there holding their bags patiently. "Um," Miles called out to her over people's heads, "do you know how many hours ahead we are from the States?" He was still trying to grasp that he was on the other side of the world.

Suddenly, the doors to the plane began to open on both sides. People began to walk off the plane on either side. Each side had three doors that led to the jetway. Miles watched in astonishment as people filed out on either side as opposed to the one exit he was accustomed to. He waited for the flight attendant to get closer to him.

"Boy, this is weird," he said as she approached. "How many hours ahead are we?"

"We are eleven hours ahead of New York," she said cheerfully. "Welcome, welcome."

"Eleven hours, OK," Miles computed in his head. "That's twelve hours my time. Ha, no wonder my watch was right." Miles was still amazed that passengers were getting off the plane through doors in the middle of the cabin. "Can we get off that way? Did something go wrong?"

"Yes, you leave this way," the woman said with a broad smile. "This way," she urged him again.

"Yep, I get it. This way. Thank you," he said in a very confused tone. "This is totally wild." Miles stepped off the plane and into the long corridor that led towards the terminal.

He could feel the outside air even though they were inside the jetway. It felt pleasantly warm. He was expecting it to be freezing cold. Then Miles remembered. "Ah, they don't do Fahrenheit over here. She meant Celsius. Feels like it's in the 70's here." Miles shook his head as he followed the other passengers towards the terminal. "Boy, they sure know how to build cities over here. Who woulda thunk it?"

As he emerged from the tunnel, his eyes grew wide as saucers. The terminal was an amazing sight and of itself. The levels seemed endless with the multitudes of people that were moving about. It was definitely at peak hour for travelers in this airport. There were people moving about without even walking, using moving sidewalks, escalators and elevators that held at least twenty or thirty people at a time. They were moving in all kinds of directions. Even those who were not on the moving sidewalks seemed to be floating by much quicker than any person could walk or run. It was truly amazing. He guessed that the levels in the rounded terminal were at least twenty stories high. He could not even take a guess as to how many gates the terminal had, but it was a very busy place indeed. Everything looked spectacular. The walls, the ceilings, the fixtures, all had a shiny glass or metallic sheen to them and looked brand new everywhere he looked.

He was overwhelmed by the spectacle of the place, and the vast numbers of people everywhere. They were all different kinds of people too, from all races and all nations. It was as if Bangkok were the central station for the entire planet. At least that's how it seemed to Miles.

He did not know where to go. He did not even know if he had booked a hotel or not. Even though he was decidedly curious about this new place, he could not help but wonder about his family back home. Did they get away from the storm? Why was he not still there helping them? Why did he have to leave so suddenly? Then he thought about his job as a software engineer. Perhaps he had been sent on business to this country? Why could he not remember?

He began to look for signs in the enormous terminal for direction. Which way to the baggage claim? How do you get to outside transportation? One thing he was definitely looking forward to was the ride to a hotel. After what he had seen from the air as they *supposedly* landed, he was quite intrigued by their mode of transport here.

He looked around for signs that were in English. They had direction signage everywhere but none of them were actually real signs. All the informational displays were not on walls or on marquees, but rather were displayed in the air. Flight information, baggage claims, ticket counter directions, transportation options; all were somehow projected high above the mass of travelers and seemed to move with you as you moved. The information was always right there where you needed it. All you had to do was look up and there was the latest flight information. To the left were directions to baggage, carports, restrooms, restaurants and many other services.

Miles stepped onto one of the moving sidewalks and looked in awe as he passed one gate after another. Soon he saw a sign that sounded good to him. It was a sign for an airport tavern just ahead called the Faraway Tavern. It was in English and he knew what it meant, and a drink sounded better than anything right now. There was no handrail for the moving sidewalk, so he just stepped off wherever he could like everyone else was doing. He approached the entrance to the bar and a projected image on the wall described the entertainment inside. The words were in several languages including English. It read: *Now playing, Trini and Tawni Nguyen, Granddaughters of the famous early twenty-first century artist, Thao Nguyen.* Miles shook his head. "Never heard of them," he laughed out loud. "Early twenty-first century, huh? No kidding, right? That's a good one."

He found an empty booth near the tiny stage where two young Asian girls were singing. They sat on old bar stools with a single microphone in front of them. He did not know which one was Trini or Tawni, but both of them looked almost identical. The girl on the left was strumming an acoustic guitar and the other just sat with her hands folded in her lap as she sang. The girl on the right had a small single drum next to her but she was not playing it. The two girls sang in high-pitched but pleasant voices. He listened to them intently and realized they were singing in English. He shrugged his shoulders. "Not bad," he said.

All-of-a-sudden, a waitress appeared out of nowhere. Miles did not even notice her approaching. She spoke to him in Thai initially and Miles looked at her confused. "I'm sorry?" he said.

"What you have?" the woman asked in broken English.

"Um, I don't know. But I need something quick. It's gotta be five o'clock somewhere, right?" Miles quipped, but the woman did not smile or laugh. He let it go. "What beers do you have on tap? Do you have a menu?"

The woman looked at him annoyed, as if he were crazy for not knowing where the menu was located. "You have," she said as she hastily swiped her hand on the table and a menu instantly popped up from out of nowhere. Miles jolted back in his chair as the menu hovered in the air before him. "You swipe each page, yeah? Beer here, food there," she spoke in a most exasperated voice. "You look. I come back. You get?" She immediately glided away from the table to another customer.

Miles stared wild-eyed as she glided away, instead of walking away. "How the hell is she doing that? It's like she's ice skating!" His hands shaking just a bit, Miles answered to himself. "Yeah, I get." He sat and stared at the floating words of the menu. He stared in amazement at the list of beers on the holographic menu. He reached his fingers towards the list and tried to touch them, but they passed right through the words. "This is freakin' cool, man." Then he remembered what she had told him. "I swipe." Placing his fingers to the right side of the hovering page, he swiped his hand to the left across the page. Instantly the next page of the menu was displayed showing all the food available at the tavern. He swiped his hand again. The last page was a more informative passage about the entertainment, Trini and Tawni Nguyen. "Ah cool," he said again as he swiped back to the front page for the beers.

Within minutes the waitress returned to take his order. "You learn menu, yeah?" she asked sarcastically.

"Yeah, it's freakin' awesome," Miles answered. The waitress was still not impressed. Miles stopped smiling and gave his order. "I'll have a pilsner." The woman immediately spun around in her hovering shoes and sped off towards the bar to retrieve his beer. Miles watched her, shaking his head at her nifty shoes. "Unbelievable how she glides like that. Viv would love those."

He observed the room as he sipped on his beer. Others in the bar were having conversations or reading the holographic menus at their table. He soon realized that the menus were more than just a menu. They were actual personal computers with access to the internet. People were reading the news and other things. "This is something else," Miles said to himself.

He decided to try it himself. Swiping his hand over the tabletop in a motion towards himself, the screen flipped out of the table into the air as if from nowhere. He examined the options on the screen. Being a software engineer, it did not take him long to learn his way around the floating device. He scrolled through headlines in English about news of the day from around Thailand and the world. Then he saw a headline about a typhoon that was approaching Taiwan. His memories started coming back just then. "Boy, I need to call Vicky," he muttered. He checked the outside of his pockets but felt nothing that resembled his phone. He even stood and searched all his pockets, his shirt pocket, everywhere. All he found in his front pants pocket was a single, shiny marble. "Cas," he said, staring at it. "You and these darn things." But his cell phone was nowhere on him. "Ah man, it must have fallen out on the plane."

He looked around the tavern thinking of what he could do. He thought of finding an information desk or ticket counter to contact the airline. *I wonder if the plane is still here. It's bound to be,* he thought to himself. He noticed a window at the end of the tavern. He knew he was fairly close to the gate where he had gotten off the plane, so he decided to take a look.

What he saw made him forget all about his phone or calling his wife. His mouth opened wide but no words could come out. Outside the terminal were airplanes coming in and going out. Except they were not taxiing on a runway; they were gliding through the air into their own parking slot. Miles could not believe what he was seeing. There were rounded docking stations ten or twelve terminals deep, and at least twenty floors high. Another line of terminals were visible several thousand yards across the way. At each floor of each terminal, there were at least five aircraft docked in a semi-circle. It was the most impressive formation of aircraft he had ever laid eyes on. Even more astonishing was watching one of the aircraft arriving at its gate. Each one slid into a slot that had a cushioned barrier on each side that also served as jetway corridors for passengers to board and disembark on. The barriers held the plane firmly and safely in place. Miles became very nervous as he watched. *How could this be? These planes aren't coming in for a landing. They are...docking.*

"No way," Miles said out loud. "There's not an aircraft around that size that can float like that. Not where I come from." His nervousness had begun to change into fear. Now he knew something was not just different here, but very wrong, too. "No commercial jet can glide like that. No way."

He went back to his beer and nervously tried to make sense of what was happening. He needed to look for clues. There had to be some way to shed some light on his situation. "Maybe I'm dreaming," he mumbled. "Maybe I got hypnotized or something. Maybe I was drugged on the plane."

Just then, the Nguyen sisters announced the next song they were going to perform. "This next song was written by our grandmother over fifty years ago. It's called *Kindness Be Conceived*. Hope you like it."

Sweat began to form on Miles' forehead. He grasped the mug of beer in both hands as the girls sang the soft little tune. Trini strummed her guitar and Tawni joined in with a soft percussion accompaniment. They sang the sweet duet, which sounded very nice to Miles even though he was extremely worried and nervous. The song had a somewhat folksy or country twang to it.

"Strange song for a couple girls from Thailand," Miles

asserted. It most certainly sounded like an American song. Then he started thinking. *Did this grandmother really compose a song like this back in the 50's?*

Suddenly he realized he had the internet right in front of him. He quickly pulled up the screen again and did a search for the song title and the grandmother's name, Thao Nguyen. Within seconds, he found what he was looking for. Sure enough, the song appeared on an album by Thao Nguyen called *We the Common*. "Well I'll be darned, there it is!" Miles exclaimed. "OK, what year? What year...?" he mumbled as he scrolled around on the web entry. He followed along the screen with his finger, reading the particulars about the album. Reading out loud, he said, "Song titles, written by, produced by, and the year released..." His finger froze in mid-air. "2013."

His blood ran cold. He had to be dreaming. This was getting too much for him to bear. "It can't be from 2013 if it's over fifty years old. This is 2005." Then he remembered something. Sweat began to drip from his face. He had never felt so emotional or scared in all his life. "This is a computer. It has to have a date." He swiped at screens, madly trying to figure out how to find the date and time. He did not have to swipe though. His eyes finally captured what they were searching for. Up in the far-right corner, in fuzzy, gleaming numbers, read the time and date: *9:43 P.M. 21/10/2065.*

Miles rubbed his eyes. "This can't be..." He looked all

around the room in desperation. He leaped from his booth and began swiping at every empty table top and reading the time and date on every screen. All of them read the same thing: *9:43 P.M. 21/10/2065.*

He stood helplessly in the middle of the terminal bar. It was then he realized that it was not a dream. He was in fact, somehow, sixty years in the future.

Chapter 2
The Pawns

Miles stood in the middle of the airport tavern, still trying to get over the shock of realizing he was in the future. Waves of emotions cascaded over him, but his family came to mind first. He could not be here in this time. He could not be in the year 2065. He had to be back with them in 2005. They needed him. Although he was fascinated and intrigued by this future city and time, he was also terrified and frightened. He had to get out of there. He had to find help. Somehow.

He left the tavern and stepped out into the busy terminal. It was still very crowded with people going every which way. Glancing up at the marquee, he saw that ground transportation was just ahead. He stepped onto the crowded moving sidewalk and was whisked away in that direction. He saw another sign for the outside terminus. He hopped off the sidewalk and made his way down another speedy escalator. It was longer than he imagined. It must have descended at least ten floors. When he reached the bottom, he knew it must be the right place. Just outside the giant entry doors to the terminal he could see the long, sleek, tubular transports that he had seen from the air. They came in all different sizes; there were some to accommodate many people and some for one or two passengers. Curling his lip, Miles uttered, "Well at least they still have buses and taxis."

Before he knew it, a young Thai man, dressed in a chauffeur's uniform and hat, approached him amongst the throng of travelers. He was holding a small tablet that scrolled a digital name over and over. Miles noticed the man out of the corner of his eye. Then astonishingly, he saw the name that was scrolling on the young man's electronic sign: *Devereaux, Miles* it read, over and over.

He did not look to be any more than eighteen years old. He had a broad smile, though, and walked right up to Miles. "You Miles?" he asked cheerfully.

Miles looked at him curiously. He was almost relieved that someone knew who he was, but also terribly puzzled as well. How would anyone know him here, in this time? It was then he knew he was here for a reason. But what? "How did you know that?" Miles inquired.

The young man laughed. "You the only one who look lost."

Miles wanted to laugh, but was still not comfortable enough to accept his new situation. He did not want to be rude, and the young man did not appear to be threatening at all. "That's an understatement, buddy. I guess I am pretty obvious." Motioning to the electronic sign, he said, "I guess you didn't need that thing."

The man laughed again. Miles found him to be very amusing right away. "Ha ha, no. But I insisted on having it. Make me look like a big shot." Miles chuckled at him. He liked his quirkiness. The man removed his hat and stuck out his hand. "I am Chen. I will escort you."

Miles shook Chen's hand. "Nice to meet you, Chen. But how…?"

"Oh, it's very nice to meet you, Mr. Miles. It is honor for me."

That remark puzzled Miles even more. How in the world could someone from the future be honored to meet him? How would he even know who he was? "An honor?" Miles asked. "I have to admit that's a first for me. No one's ever told me that. And you can just call me Miles."

"Oh, no problem, Mr. Miles. My honor, as I say."

Miles shook his head. He just let it go. He was simply happy to be speaking to someone who knew him. "So, what now, Chen?"

Chen placed his hat back on his head. "I escort you.

Come, come."

The little man led him through the crowds of people and through the vast doors of the terminal. There were more projected signs outside and transports everywhere. Even though it appeared to be chaotic, it was actually very organized. People lined along the curb and boarded transports one by one. As quickly as they boarded, they were soon off on their way, and quite fast, as well. Each vehicle took off in a *whoosh*, one by one, in an organized, efficient and speedy manner that would impress a general. It was not long before Miles noticed that these vehicles did not appear to have wheels at all. Somehow they glided across the smooth surface of the road.

"Hey, Chen!" he called over the busy scene. "Is it me or do these things not have any wheels?"

Chen began to laugh heartily. "No, no wheels, Mr. Miles. No wheels for long time now. Before I born. These GG transport. Very efficient. The whole world learn from us."

"A what?" Miles asked.

Before he got an answer, Chen was leading him to the curb. "We next. Be ready."

"Oh, okay. Sure." Miles' hands began to shake. He tried to calm himself and his thoughts. *It's just a ride you idiot. Relax.*

Within seconds, a small transport built for two people pulled up and stopped without much of a noise at all. Miles was amazed at how quiet these GG cars were. A door slid open with a swishing sound. Miles climbed into one of the bucket seats. It was very comfortable and made of the finest leather. Then something else alarmed him and made him even more nervous.

"Chen, there's nobody driving this thing." He noticed that Chen was not getting inside the vehicle. "Hey, aren't you getting in to drive this thing? I don't know what to do, there's no damn steering wheel!"

Peering just inside the car, Chen answered, "Relax, Mr. Miles. It drive for you. Enjoy Bangkok." Then, looking at the front control panel, Chen issued a command in Thai, "Chatuchak," and without warning the door swished shut.

"Hey, wait a minute," Miles blurted out. Before he could say anymore, the car sped away from the airport, leaving Chen behind on the curb.

Miles took a deep breath as the car picked up speed. He could not tell how fast he was going, but he knew it was easily more than the normal sixty-five he was used to back in 2005. He was astonished at how fast and quiet the little car performed. He was very curious as to what the term GG meant. The car went over hills and curbs effortlessly, barely slowing down for each one. Soon, it began to ascend a steep hill, but the speed remained constant. The angle of the climb became steeper and steeper and Miles began to worry. "Whoa…" Miles said out loud. He checked to make sure his seat belt was fastened. Suddenly, his seat automatically began to adjust its position so that Miles was not laying on his back but sitting upright as the vehicle turned completely vertical and continued on its climb at the same speed. It was ascending the side of a building just like an elevator. "Oh man! This is wild!" Even the sides of buildings were part of the highway infrastructure. As the car rose, the view of the night skyline was amazing. Miles was stunned as a passing vehicle went by in the other direction. "Geez," he yelled and glued his hands to both sides of his seat. Soon the car curved to the left and leveled out once again. At the same time, his chair adjusted automatically so that he was sitting upright as normal in the fascinating vehicle. "Wow, I've got to get me one of these."

"Good evening, Mr. Devereaux," a female computer voice greeted. Miles jumped in his seat, not expecting to hear a voice when he was the only one in the car. "Welcome. It is a pleasure to meet you." The voice was very pleasant and polite.

Miles adjusted a bit in his seat, realizing it was a robotic device within the car. "Right back at ya." He glanced around the front and the back of the car to see if there was a face to go with the voice. At this point, he was ready for anything, but he saw nothing. "Well, you know who I am. What do I call you? You got a name?"

"Of course. I am GG 42-7." For a robotic voice, it was

very personable. "I am delighted to be your assistant this evening as well as your personal mode of transport."

"Well, thank you, GG 42 whatever you said."

"GG 42-7."

"Gotcha. I wasn't expecting a personal assistant." Miles tried to think of something else to say. "So, what's GG stand for anyway? Do you know?"

"Oh yes, Mr. Devereaux. It means Gravity Glider, Model 42-7," she said politely.

"Oh, of course," Miles replied, rolling his eyes. "What's a Gravity Glider?"

"It's the type of vehicle you are riding in at the moment, Mr. Devereaux."

"Just call me Miles."

"Of course, Miles," she answered.

Miles scratched his chin. He finally got his name straightened out. He did not like being so formal, even if it was a robot. "So, what should I call you? Glider Gal?"

"You can call me GG 42-7."

"No, that's too formal," Miles persisted. "How about… Gigi?"

"That will be acceptable."

"Great! Glad we got that out of the way." He thought about how Gigi described the vehicles name. "So, we are actually gliding in this thing?"

"Precisely."

"How?"

"By the power-generating electro-pulsars located on the under-carriage of this vessel, of course," Gigi said matter-of-factly. "They push against the Earth's gravity, thus causing the transport to glide at exactly 0.43 meters above the surface. Thus, we are able to glide."

Miles nodded in understanding. "And how do we accelerate? What makes this thing go? Sorry for all the questions, but I'm an engineer and I'm very curious. Plus, I'm uh…new in town."

"Curiosity is one of my sub-routines," Gigi replied. "So, I am completely understanding."

"That's terrific. How's this thing move if we're gliding?" Miles was getting a bit impatient. He wanted to learn as much as he could about the future. It was truly fascinating to him.

"By the wave-flux thrusters, of course."

"Oh, of course. Excuse me for asking," Miles said sarcastically.

"Don't mention it."

"I guess sarcasm is one of your sub-routines as well?"

Gigi answered at once. "I have thousands of sub-routines programmed into my interface."

Miles nodded. He knew that Gigi must be incredibly intelligent, but only because of what humans had programmed her with. Despite that, she was still someone to talk to, and she took his mind off his current dilemma: how to get back home. "Well, how about humor? Is that one of them, too?"

"Oh yes, Miles. I enjoy a good humorous anecdote."

"Well, I don't know about you bartender, but this cowpoke could use a drink."

"A reference to the American Old West from the nineteenth century, is it not?"

"Bingo."

Gigi continued, "I have analyzed your DNA on the armrest and have determined you have consumed only 0.265 ounces of alcohol in the past ninety minutes. You are allowed another drink at this time."

Miles looked down at his armrest. How did she know that his DNA was on the armrest? He was truly fascinated.

"The sweat from your palms formed a residue that I am able to examine," Gigi explained.

"How did you know what I was curious about?" Miles inquired.

"I saw you look at your armrest."

"Wait, you can see me?"

"Of course, Miles. I am all around you."

"Well, why can't I see you?" Miles protested. "It's not really fair y'know. I feel like I'm talking to a ghost. It's kinda startin' to creep me out."

"Very well, Miles." Instantly a female face appeared in mid-air in the front of the vehicle. A young woman with dark hair and plain features with a fair complexion smiled broadly at him. She did not appear Asian in appearance as he had expected, but more European. What was more striking was how familiar her face seemed to him. He could not quite put his finger on why but in any case, a friendly face was just fine with him.

"Wow. Um, hi. I wasn't expecting that." Miles was clearly taken off guard again. "Nice to see you."

"It's nice to be seen," Gigi replied. "Now, were you still desiring to have a drink?"

"Um, well," Miles stammered. He was still a bit taken aback now that he was actually talking to a real face. At least a virtual one. "That was actually a joke."

"I did recognize the humor in your request. However, you may have a drink if you wish. It is my desire to assist in your comfort in any way."

"Well, if you put it that way, I'll have a gin and tonic with a squeeze of lime." Miles was not too confident she would actually produce a drink for him in the vehicle but he was willing to believe anything at this point.

"Shaken or stirred?" she asked.

"You pick. I don't care," Miles replied sheepishly. Within seconds, a tray appeared from a hidden compartment in front of him and a glass filled with a gin and tonic over ice and a slice of lime wedged on the rim appeared from a hole in the tray. Then a napkin slid out from another unknown slot and slid perfectly onto the tray next to his glass. "Unbelievable. Um... thanks."

"My pleasure, Miles."

Miles examined the glass with a smile. He shook his head and squeezed the lime juice into his drink. After wiping his fingers on the napkin, he lifted the glass and toasted, "Here's mud in your eye!"

"They are not real eyes, Miles."

He took a long swig form his glass. "I guess they don't have that one in your sub-routines. Just kidding, Gigi ol' pal."

The car began to slow and Miles tried to read the projected road signs along the highway. All of the signs were in four languages at all times with English being the second one listed. Thai was listed first and he could make out some Spanish on the third line. He could not tell what the fourth language was on each sign, though. As the car slowed, he noticed another sign that read Chatuchak Market in English. For whatever reason, this appeared to be the destination Chen had chosen for Miles. He finished his drink as the car came to a complete stop.

"We are here, Miles," Gigi informed him.

Miles frowned a bit. He was not expecting to go shopping at this late hour. His world was completely turned on end and all he wanted to do was rest and think of a way to get back to his own time. "We're going to a market? How about just a nice hotel and a hot shower?"

Gigi ignored him, however. "First we must get you prepared. You can't go dressed the way you are. They will never respect you."

Miles looked down at his clothing. He was still wearing the old clothes he had thrown on the day before when he was still in 2005. "You have a dress code for an open-air market, do ya? Well this is all I have, my holographic pal. I seem to be traveling light on this trip. So, this is it I'm afraid and I sure ain't going naked." Miles thought for another second on the other thing she had just said. "Who are *they*?"

"Let me worry about your attire, Miles. Reach inside the seat pocket in front of you," she instructed him. "You will find a communicator device, or CommVice." Miles reached his hand inside the pocket in front of him and produced a small watch-like device. "Wear it on your wrist so you can take me with you after you exit the glider."

As soon as Miles put on the CommVice, Gigi's face instantly disappeared from inside the glider and appeared in smaller form, hovering just above the device on his wrist. Miles laughed at its simplicity and marveled at its ingenuity. "Incredible."

"Are you ready, Miles?" Gigi asked.

Miles curled his lower lip. He did not really want to play

tourist, but who was he to ask questions? "The lady wants to go shopping. So, let's go shopping. Lead on McDuff."

"I thought we had agreed upon calling me Gigi," she immediately countered.

"Yeah, yeah. Let's go," Miles droned. *No sense in trying to explain quips to a futuristic hologram,* he thought.

As Miles reached to open the door, it opened on its own. "OK, so the doors open themselves, too." As soon as he stepped out of the glider, his clothes transformed completely. Gone were the old ratty blue jeans and drab button down shirt from the past. Instantly he was wearing a stylish, new white shirt and beige trousers with a sport coat. It was a familiar fashion but still something he had never seen before. He looked down at himself in amazement. "Whoa," was all he could say. "How the hell…"

Giving her approval, Gigi simply replied, "That's better. Now we can go."

Miles was still a bit startled. "Um, yeah. Let's uh…let's go." As he walked towards the market, he continued to look his new instant clothes over in astonishment. "That's some trick, Gigi."

"Thank you."

At the entrance to the street-side market was an ancient statue of the Buddha. It was faded and dark gray. The statue was no more than a few feet high and the depiction was of a sitting Buddha, cross-legged in a meditative pose. His head was adorned with a perfectly carved beaded cap. Miles was impressed with the artistry of the old statue. Countless people walked in and out of the market past the seemingly unnoticed monument. Miles remembered from his studies that this part of the world mostly practiced Buddhism. He thought that statues such as this must be quite common everywhere.

Even though it was late in the evening, the market was abuzz with people everywhere. There were rows and rows of vendors selling anything you could think of. There were tables full of leather goods, clothing, household goods, kitchen tools, fine china, works of art, fresh fruits and vegetables, and even live animals. There was also an enormous section dedicated to hot food and refreshments. Being on the coast, the food market was a choice place for people looking to buy fresh seafood. There were fish of all varieties stacked on packs of ice everywhere. A fresh smell of seafood wafted throughout the food market. Miles had been to many farmers' markets back home but never had he seen one this large and elaborate.

"This is the largest and busiest market in Thailand," Gigi said proudly.

Miles glanced down at his wrist and responded flatly, "Yeah, no kidding." As he looked around the market at all the different people milling about shopping, he noticed that a great deal of the people did not look Asian at all. In fact, most of the people looked like Americans or at least Westerners. "Geez, sure are a lot of tourists here." He scanned over the leather goods in one section. It was full of purses and pocketbooks.

"Do you see anything that you like?" asked Gigi.

Miles nodded. "Well, if I had any money, I'd probably get Vicky a souvenir." Then he remembered something. "Oh man, come to think of it I'm not even sure I paid for that beer back at the airport. Oh crap."

"Do not worry. I took care of that," Gigi responded.

Miles lifted his wrist to his face. "You took care of it? But how did…"

Gigi cut him off. "Do you see anything she would like?" They were standing before a stall dedicated to small pieces of art and jewelry. They were everywhere, perfectly aligned on tables and hanging on the interior walls. As he looked around, he noticed that not just this vendor, but all the vendors in this section sold the same thing. There was row after row of these vendors. He could not believe how many there were.

"Wow! What are all these little trinkets?" Miles asked.

Gigi quickly answered, as if she were a travel guide. "These are some of the most prized and holiest treasures in Bangkok. These are known as *pra*, or in your language, a talisman."

"Talisman?" he asked quizzically.

"Yes. Or in a simpler term, an amulet," she answered.

"Ah, I see." He looked around at the vast array and nodded his head. "Yeah, this would probably be a good thing for her. She would like this." He shook his head at the vast number of choices. He did not know how to decide which one would be the best. "But there are so many. How does one begin to choose?"

Gigi replied, "The most valuable are not necessarily the best. A *pra* is best suited for what you desire. One does not buy amulets. One simply borrows or rents them. Each amulet here has been hand carved or formed by monks and handed down or traded over many years and decades. There are amulets that are meant for those seeking wealth or good fortune, or those seeking protection or guidance." Miles stood before a table full of shiny and polished amulets. "However, the ones that are nice and shiny are newer and do not have the same kind of luck as the old ones. The dirtier and older they are, the better."

"Is that right?" Miles was very impressed. He moved along to look more closely at the amulets that were older and dirtier in appearance. Many had the image of Buddha, but others had depictions of monkeys, elephants, or buffaloes. He began to notice that some also had pictures of people on them. Perhaps they were owned by families who carried pictures of their loved ones this way.

He walked slowly as he scanned over each table full of amulets. Finally, one in particular caught his eye. Miles froze.

For some reason he could not take his eyes off of it. The amulet was made of silver and was badly tarnished and black. It appeared to be quite old. In the center was a faded photo of a young girl, perhaps twelve to fifteen years of age. She had dark hair and eyes, and just a slight hint of a smile on her face. She looked strikingly familiar to Miles, yet a much younger version. He could not think of who the little girl reminded him of, but still he could not take his eyes off her. The old man behind the counter noticed the amulet Miles was staring at and gladly picked it up for him with his old, leathery hands.

"Come, come," the man said. "This one, you." He placed the amulet in Miles' hand and closed his fingers around it. As soon as he placed it in Miles' hand, eight darkened figures rose in unison from behind the tables across the aisle behind him. He had not noticed them, though. They were all the same height and all dressed the same. All of them were wearing darkened shades and dressed in shiny black body suits. The only difference was each had their own bright, neon color stripe running the length of their suits on each side. There was simmering red, electric flame, tangerine orange, emerald green, metallic blue, neon yellow, sharp turquoise and glowing maroon. Unbeknownst to Miles, stood the near identical, expressionless, hoods, all in a row.

Miles smiled back at the man and nodded. He opened his hand and examined the amulet closer. The faded photo was under a rounded glass cover. The glass was faded with age, yet he could still see the plain face of the little girl. Her eyes seemed to be staring directly back at him. "What an amazing face! It's like I've seen it before or something." Neither Gigi nor the old man said anything. Miles flipped the amulet over. The back was even darker with tarnish. He glided his finger slowly across the back and found engraved markings on it. He wiped it with his fingers and looked closer, trying to decipher what the markings were. He pulled his shirt tail out and tried to polish it. He then stepped back into the main aisle to get more light. "You mind?" he asked the old man. He just smiled and nodded. Miles held the amulet closer to the light and finally saw that the markings were actually letters. "G.B.," Miles said softly. He flipped it back over and looked at the picture again. "Probably her initials, you think Gigi?"

Gigi answered, "It is a possibility, Miles. Monks never signed their work so it is quite possible the previous caretaker of this item engraved letters on it."

At that moment, Miles turned and noticed the eight figures behind the kiosks across from him. He became uneasy when he saw them. They did not look like any of the other vendors in the market. Suddenly, all in a line, the young teens began to glide away down the row. They glided and crisscrossed between the tables and the main aisle in perfect unison. Miles was bewildered as he watched them glide effortlessly away, just like the waitress in the tavern. He shook his head and walked back into the stall where the old man was waiting.

"That was weird," Miles blurted. "Crazy kids." He turned his attention back to the old man. "I like this one but I don't know how to pay for it."

The man motioned to Miles' wrist, but Miles did not understand. "Raise your CommVice to him," Gigi instructed.

"Oh," Miles said and clumsily lifted his arm. The man quickly scanned the device and smiled in appreciation. "Thank you. Thank you very much. I guess this is my credit card." Miles chuckled nervously to himself. He turned to leave but the old man grabbed his arm.

"Come, come," he said. He reached under the table and produced a small chain on which to put the amulet so one could wear it.

"Oh, thanks again. I guess I do need a chain for it." Miles took the chain and slid it through the tiny loop on the top of the amulet. He balled it up in his hand and waved goodbye to the man.

"No," the man insisted, "You wear." He motioned for Miles to put it on.

"Sure, sure. You want me to put it on? Yeah, sure." Miles clasped the chain behind his neck and he admired the amulet as it hung just over his shirt collar. "How do I look?"

"Good, good," the old man said satisfied.

Miles continued to walk through the crowded market wearing his 'new' amulet. The crowds began to die down and he noticed some vendors were beginning to close their stalls. "Well, Gigi, you had enough? What's next? Have I earned a hot shower and soft bed yet?"

"As they say in the West, Miles, the night is still young," Gigi quipped. "We're just getting started."

Miles shook his head as he neared the exit to the street. "I appreciate the thought, and you're a swell date and all, but it is getting pretty late isn't it? And what do you mean just getting started? Getting started with what?"

At the very moment he reached the exit, instead of seeing the busy street where they parked, he was instantly transported. Miles was stunned to find himself in a blaring, darkened and very crowded nightclub.

"Whoa! What happened?" Miles shouted over the loud music. "How the hell did we get here? Where's the freakin' car?" Miles was shaken by the instant change. He looked around nervously at the crowded nightspot. "What is this, some kind of club?"

"Precisely," Gigi said. "Beats driving, doesn't it?"

"Whoa, whoa, slow down. This isn't normal. How did we get from the market to here just like that?"

"Relax, Miles," Gigi assured him. "Enjoy the music, enjoy the dancing. Have a drink. Your alcohol level is still well below acceptable."

"Yeah, yeah, whatever. A drink sounds perfect. That's exactly what I need, a freakin' drink!" He thought for a moment as he collected himself. Sweat began to bead on his forehead. *How could this be happening?* His mind raced. "Wait, wait. Forget the drink. I need some air. Can we go outside please? Just for a minute?"

"This way," Gigi guided.

As he moved through the throng of people on the upper levels of the club, he looked down at the main dance floor far below. Again, he noticed that most of the people in the club looked to be Americans. He figured the local establishments had to keep the tourists happy with all the hotspots and entertainment. He people-watched from the edge of the railing. Cheerful partiers danced in unison to the blaring, yet catchy music. It was music like he had ever heard before. He was impressed at how in sync all the dancers were. It was really cool to watch.

He found the door to a balcony outside. People were milling about and talking outside, away from the loud music. Miles made his way over to the railing. The view was spectacular. He had never seen such an amazing city skyline. It was clearly impressive with the colorful lights and incredible shiny and spotless skyscrapers everywhere. He guessed they were at least five floors up. Gliders zipped by down below on the streets and up the sides of buildings just like elevators. It was most definitely the future, and Miles was constantly amazed by it.

"Geez, doesn't this city ever sleep?" he asked bewildered.

"Of course, not, Miles," she answered. "But the people do."

"Very funny."

"Welcome to Sukhumvit district," Gigi said. "The hottest nightlife around."

Miles shook his head in amazement. "Fascinating. Simply fascinating." As he gazed at the bright lights of the Bangkok skyline, he began to feel uneasy. His thoughts returned to his wife and children back home in another time. The time where he belonged. He tried to remember what was happening before he awoke on the plane, but still his mind was not clear. He could not understand why. He shook his head as his frustration grew.

"Is something the matter, Miles?" his virtual friend asked.

He pursed his lips and answered, saying, "You mean besides how weird it looks for me being the only one on this deck that is talking to his wrist?" In a split second, Gigi appeared before him in full form. Miles stood dumbfounded still holding his wrist upward. He blinked his eyes hoping that it was just an illusion, but it was not. Gigi stood before him, only a few inches shorter than he was. What fascinated him the most was how natural she looked. He held his hands up and exclaimed, "OK, so nobody out here noticed that? Am I the only one that finds this totally freaking cool? How did you do that?"

"I am able to transform to fit your particular communication needs, Miles."

"It's so weird!" Miles exclaimed. He slowly walked around her as if she were a piece of furniture. "You sure you are a hologram? You look so real! I thought maybe you would be all pixelated and stuff like on Star Wars or something." He reached out to touch her shoulder but stopped his hand. "Do you mind?" Gigi shrugged her shoulders. He reached his hand out to place it on her shoulder but it went right through it as if it were a liquid. He felt nothing solid, yet a tingly sensation ran through his fingers and his hand. "Whoa. That's the most awesome thing I have ever seen or felt." He realized how it must look to the other patrons on the balcony and quickly pulled his hand back.

"Don't worry, Miles. People in this time are quite used to holograms. They are not even paying attention to us." Miles froze when he heard these words. He stared at her silently as he became even more nervous. It was the first time she had acknowledged that his situation was not quite right.

"People in this time?" Miles hissed under breath. Gigi watched him as if she were waiting for him to fill in the blanks. "So, you know then? You know this is the year 2065?"

"Of course I do," she answered succinctly.

"Then you know I don't belong here, right?" Gigi remained silent. "Gigi, please. You gotta help me. I don't know how I got here. I don't know why I am here. And I definitely don't know how I can get back." Gigi still said nothing. She just stood there listening to him, staring at him blankly. Miles was about to burst as he tried helplessly to probe her for answers. He paced around in front of her, wiping his chin as he tried to think. "Why aren't you saying anything? You know something, don't you? Please, tell me what's going on?"

"Where do you belong?" Gigi finally asked.

Before he could answer, it became apparent that they were the only ones on the balcony. Everyone had left and Miles had not even noticed it; everyone except for one person standing in front of the balcony door leading back inside the club. It was one of the young kids dressed in black that he had seen at the market. A metallic, emerald green stripe ran the length of her skin-tight suit on either side. She stood defiantly in front of the door facing Miles with her dark shades on. "Hey," Miles called out, "I've seen you before! What do you want?"

The young girl yelled something at him in Thai. He did not know what she said but it definitely sounded threatening. Miles' eyes grew wide as the girl made a series of martial arts moves. Within a split second she hurled a ninja star directly at Miles' head. Instinctively, and with incredible reflexes, Miles dodged the razor-edged star and it went sailing over the balcony. He had not even noticed that Gigi had disappeared as well.

"Holy *shit*," Miles yelled. The young girl yelled in frustration and ran inside the club. What was surprising to Miles was that instead of being afraid for his life, his parental instincts seemed to be more attuned to what was happening than anything else. "Oh, no you don't young lady. Come back here." Miles took off after her and ran inside the club. Gone were the throngs of party goers. The massive club was entirely empty, yet the music continued to blare. The large multi-level club was still dark and colored lights continued to blink and sway all around the area and the dance floor below. The dance floor had a checkerboard look to it and each tile blinked on and off in unison with the music. He looked everywhere for the green-striped girl, but she was nowhere to be seen.

He ran down the staircases leading to the bottom floor. He looked down at his CommVice on his wrist. "Gigi, where the hell did you go? What the hell is this?" He could sense he was being watched as the music blared, but he still could not see anyone. Out of the corner of his eye, way across the lengthy main hall and dance floor, he saw a flash of the neon green suit. Miles dashed out across the dancefloor and had made it almost to the middle when he froze in his tracks. Suddenly the music changed to a distinctive song. It sounded familiar but Miles was certain he had never heard it before. What made him freeze was not the music but the second it had changed, his clothes changed too! Miles looked down at himself. He was no longer wearing the casual sport coat and slacks. He was dressed in his own black body suit. A single stripe of majestic neon purple ran down his arms only.

"Oh crap, not again," Miles said out loud. "I do look pretty badass though, I'll have to admit."

As the song began to play, he noticed that he was no longer alone on the checkerboard dance floor. The eight hooligans were back, all aligned perfectly surrounding him on the flashing dancefloor. They still wore their shades and all were dressed in black with their distinctive neon stripes. They began to glide and circle him. Their expressionless faces stared at him through their shades. Miles marveled at how they glided in their shoes, as if they were ice skates. Their feet barely touched the floor as they circled.

The music was hypnotic. It was as if they were putting him into a trance with it. It was slow and methodical but still had a catchy beat. He tried to move and keep a close eye on them as they circled but his feet felt funny. He could not turn the way he wanted to. He looked down at his feet and saw that he was wearing the same kind of shoes as the kids. He tried to step and turn but his feet never touched the floor. Before he knew it he slipped under his own weight and went crashing to the floor. "What the hell? These shoes don't touch the *floor*." He tried desperately to stand and keep his eye on the circling gang. He suddenly saw Gigi standing just above them behind a railing on the next level. "Gigi? What are these stupid shoes? I can't freakin' stand up."

"Gravity gliders," Gigi called out. "Learn to use them quickly."

"Just like on the car?" Miles yelled back. He was frantically trying to stand. "Use them? *How?*"

The kids began to glide closer to him as if they were sharks closing in on their prey. "How do I use them, Gigi?" Miles yelled again in a sarcastic tone. "They're getting *closer*. I'm going to *die*."

"Don't rush your feet down, ease them down," Gigi finally answered.

Miles understood and slowly eased his foot down and it firmly rested on the floor. He finally stood on his one foot and then eased the other to the floor as well. "OK, I am standing up. *Finally.* Now how the hell do I move? Do I have the flux thingy's or *what?*"

"Come on, Miles. Start moving, defend yourself. Or they will lose all respect for you," Gigi warned.

"I think that time came and went, Gigi. How do I *move?*"

Gigi finally relented. "Lean with your toes. Stop and turn with your heels, dummy. Now *move*."

Miles quickly thought back to his days when he used to roller skate. He thought of how the skates had a toe stopper that could be used to push off and to stop. He figured he could use the same principal with the gravity gliders. He lifted his right foot and placed the toe on end. He gave a slight push and with that he was gliding across the lighted floor. "Holy...*crap*," he yelled out. He went flying towards some tables. "How do I turn? *How do I turn?"* He remembered what Gigi had just said. Just before he went slamming into the tables, he yelled out, "*Heel.*" He planted both feet back on the heels and he instantly stopped. He placed his right foot again on the toe and he spun around to face the kids. "Now let's see how I can turn." He pushed off again and easily glided back out onto the floor, but before he could try turning, the kid in tangerine orange sideswiped him. He quickly changed direction to the left. Another in maroon hit him again sending him in the other direction. He was about to lose control when he began to feel how the shoes responded when his feet turned. It started to become easier to control as the memory of how to skate came flooding back to his senses. He sailed towards the edge of the floor but was able to skid to a stop on his heel. He nodded in recognition. "Yeah, I got this now. Now what's with you kids?"

The music was catchy and rhythmic. The eight kids began to glide in unison and in sync to the music and continued to stare at Miles. He had never heard the music before but the rhythm was almost hypnotic. Miles stared back at them. It was as if they were dancing for him instead of making threatening gestures. He kept expecting more ninja stars to start flying at his head, but instead they just moved to the music. He glided back and forth as if he were pacing, still trying to get the feel for how to use the gravity gliders. He still had no idea what was going on.

"What are you kids doing?" he yelled at them. "What do you want from me?"

With that, the kids stopped moving to the music and began circling again. The girl in simmering red stopped on her heel and yelled out in Thai, just like the girl in green had done before and hurled something towards Miles. It was not a razor star this time. He ducked again and a flash of electric sparks struck the wall behind him. When she missed she took off right towards him. He quickly raced away from her and soon all of them were after him.

"Me and my big mouth," Miles muttered as he sped away, trying to elude them.

They all started hurling flashes of light at Miles. Each one missed and struck walls, railings, and chairs around him with a barrage of sparks. He did not know what exactly they were throwing but he could tell it probably did not feel good if one of them hit him. Miles became more adept at gliding in the shoes and he was doing well to elude them. Then, suddenly one struck him in the arm, the other in his leg. A shockwave went through his body with each strike. He yelled out in pain but was still able to keep his balance. The shock only lasted a few seconds but it was certainly effective. He frantically looked for a way to escape the nightclub. He raced from one level to the next while his pursuers kept up the chase.

"Gigi, I could use a way out of here!" he yelled out. She was nowhere to be seen again. "Any bright ideas? They're lighting me up like a *Christmas* tree."

He could not shake them though. Each level he jumped to, they were right on his tail, hurling one electric ball after another at him. He still could not find a way out. He decided to head back down to the main floor and look for an exit there. Wave after wave of electric sparks flew at him, as he raced down staircases and corridors in the seemingly endless club.

He reached the bottom and slipped behind a column and skidded to a stop. He surveyed the lower level, looking for an exit door. Soon, he spotted one on the opposite side of the checkered dancefloor. One by one the black and neon clad teens raced across the floor past the column where Miles hid. They immediately sensed he was hiding and peeled off in two circular patterns to the left and right. Miles saw his chance and went racing through the opening between the two circling groups right down the middle of the floor. He thought he was going to make it, but the second he reached the center of the floor he instantly appeared outside.

He had teleported to another part of the city. He looked all around to see if they were behind him, but they were not. He looked around in desperation trying to figure out where he was, but it did not look familiar at all. It appeared to be a town square.

Sweat poured from his face as he stood in the square looking around. "I guess I should get used to that happening by now," he said sarcastically to himself. He wiped the sweat from his forehead. "But I'm not." He kept looking all around the square, expecting to have a ball of electricity or a ninja star come flying at him at any second. But the gang of teens was not around. The square was large and open. In the middle stood a large red two-columned wooden frame that was easily over a hundred feet tall. It stood on a rounded concrete pedestal with each leg of the structure about ten to fifteen feet apart. "What the heck is that?" Miles asked out loud.

Across the square was a very large and ornate building that looked ancient and very important. "Wonder what that building is?" It was beautifully decorated and the roof had multiple tiers of green and dark red. It was obvious the architecture was Asian in style. Miles assumed it was a structure of great importance and possibly a historic site, but the large structure in the middle of the square was the most curious thing to him. He glided across the square to get a closer look at it and the building across the street.

"This is pretty interesting," he commented. He found a sign near the street between the square and the historic building hovering in the air. It was in several languages including English. He read it out loud, "Wat Suthat and Giant Swing." He looked up at the aging wooden structure in the center and asked, "That thing is a swing? Way cool. Wonder if you can try it." Miles chuckled. "Viv would love this thing." Then he read the description of the building across from the square. It was an ancient royal Buddhist temple that was over two centuries old. The façade was intricate with what looked like flutes of fire rising from the roof's edges. It was the most incredible sight he had seen thus far in his odyssey.

He stood between the two ancient structures marveling at them. The night air was warm. The salty ocean scent wafted into his nostrils. A moment of peace fell over him. He could not describe it. He looked up again at the Giant Swing, thinking of how his young daughter would be begging him to swing on it. He chuckled to himself. Oh, how he missed his family. It had only been hours since he had last seen them, but to Miles, it seemed an eternity.

Then something caught his eye. He quickly forgot about the Giant Swing and he stopped smiling. As if from nowhere, eight bright shiny orbs, floating in mid-air, appeared in the center of the square in a large circle. They glowed in golden and emerald hues in the dimly lit square. They were no bigger than softballs. In the center of the orb ring floated an even larger one. It too glowed gold and emerald, but also contained a brilliant hint of red. It was about the size of a bowling ball and floated silently in the center of the smaller orbs. Miles stood speechless as he stared at them. He knew they were not there moments before. His hands began to tremble. The sight was incredible, but he felt uneasy about it. He sensed he was being watched.

His senses were right on target. Without warning, just beyond the ring of orbs, the eight young kids appeared in a row, still dressed in black with their eight separate yet dazzling set of colors. Miles straightened himself and raised his head high in defiance. "Haven't you kids had enough fun for one night?" he asked in the most parental voice he could muster. They stood motionless and without response. He could tell that tone was not working, so he tried sarcasm. "And isn't it past your bedtimes anyway? I mean really, what is it? After midnight already?" He raised his eyebrows a bit in trying to make his point, but it was obviously not working.

Suddenly, he heard a familiar voice from across the square to his right. He instantly knew who it was. "Miles Devereaux," Gigi firmly and loudly called out. "Where do you belong?" Her voice boomed across the darkened square. He felt his blood run cold through his veins at the sound of it. Gone was the friendly tone he had grown accustomed to. Miles looked over to see Gigi standing in full form just above the square. Her voice raised in an even more commanding tone. "For you do *not* belong here."

At that instant, the eight black clad teens began to advance on Miles. They floated towards him in rapid sync. Only the ring of orbs stood between him and his pursuers. "Gigi," Miles shouted back. "Whose side are you on?"

But Gigi was the least of his worries. The kids made a beeline towards the floating orbs and Miles realized then they must be some sort of weapon. It was obvious they wanted them. Miles quickly raced towards them as well and began to circle the ring. He tried to guard them but the kids were too fast for him. He kept one eye on them and one on the orbs. He wondered what would happen if he tried to touch any of the glowing orbs. As the eight approached the circle they split off in fours to surround the ring and Miles. One by one, each skater raced towards the ring and snatched up the smaller orbs. Instantly one, two, three were gone. Miles knew he had to grab at least one or two or he would be overwhelmed by whatever force they contained. Four, five and six were captured. Miles skidded to a stop. Two orbs remained and only seconds remained before the last two kids would capture them. Then quickly he shot a glance towards the largest orb in the center.

Gigi immediately warned, "You may not touch the center

orb until all the outer markers are detonated."

Miles made a dash for the remaining two outer markers. He and the other two chasers closed in on them simultaneously. Right as it appeared he would lose them, Miles did what he felt in his instincts. He raced forward and in one final lunge, he bounced off one foot and leaped several feet into the air, flipping over the two remaining orbs and grabbed them one in each hand while he was inverted. The two kids looked on stunned as Miles flew over them. Before they could stop they crashed directly into each other and fell to the ground in a heap. Miles swirled over and landed on his glider and instantly snapped his heel down to skid to a stop. It was an incredible move.

Miles was impressed with himself. He could not believe what he had done. He nodded in approval. "Not bad. I think I got the hang of these shoes."

Suddenly, a flash of light came towards his head. He instinctively ducked as, what sounded like a huge hornet, came buzzing over his head. The sound of the flying orb was terrifying. Miles looked over his shoulder to see the zipping light smash into the concrete pedestal of the Giant Swing. The impact caused a life-sized sphere of glowing bars to spring from the middle and encircle whatever lay trapped within.

Sweat poured down Miles' face. "Ooo-kay...mental note on that one. That's what they can do, huh?" He watched as the other five kids planned their next attack on him. They circled and crisscrossed back and forth. Miles stood and quickly thought of his next move. The two that had run into each other were still on the ground but trying to get up. Miles instinctively hurled one of the orbs right between them. Instantly the orb buzzed through the air and detonated in a brilliant flash of light. A glowing sphere zapped around them in microseconds. The two were trapped helplessly inside. "I'm done with you two," Miles smartly said.

He only had one orb left though and six more chasers who had five detonators themselves. Miles took off across the square. All he could do was make them chase him and try to duck out of the way of buzzing orbs any way he could. He kept low to the ground as he skated, clutching his only weapon like a football. "You guys wanna play ball, then let's play," he muttered. He knew they were right on his tail, so he turned and pivoted on his heel. Just as he did, another orb came whizzing by just missing his head. A flashing light burst as it crashed into a park bench. "That's three," Miles said to himself. He looked up to see the six come charging straight at him. Miles took off right towards them just like a running back. Before they could hurl their weapons at him, Miles was barreling underneath them like a bull. Three of the kids went sailing over him but landed squarely on their gliders and skidded and turned back towards him. Miles headed for the Giant Swing to try and bounce off the concrete pedestal. The first cage was still glowing next to it as he skipped up the steps.

Just as he landed another orb came right at his chest. He instinctively used his sphere to block it. Fully expecting them both to detonate, Miles was stunned to see that the orb bounced off the one in his hands. The force of the impact drove the orb straight up in the air. Miles caught it with his outstretched hand. "Holy crap," he yelled. "That was nice." He immediately side-armed it towards one kid, and with a snap and a zip she was ensnared. As he took off, Miles shouted towards his latest capture, "Didn't they teach you dodgeball in school, kid? Ha ha."

Miles raced towards the other side of the square again. The kids were in hot pursuit. He knew what to listen for now. As soon as he heard the sound of a buzzing hornet, he would reach out his own orb to try and bat it away. One flew by, then another. Miles dodged the first one and then turned to knock the other one away in the nick of time. Both detonated on the hard surface and the kids skated in between each glowing cage and stayed hot on his tail. He knew they only had one more detonator and he remembered the larger center orb. He wondered what it might do if it were detonated. *If it was larger, it could not be good*, he thought to himself.

Then Miles noticed something and he began to slow down. He kept a watchful eye on his attackers and their final detonator. The previous glowing cages began to crackle and pop. The energy they used to create and hold the bars began to run out. Soon each cage began to disappear one by one all around the square. The two girls that were trapped together were freed and then the other one trapped by herself was freed. Miles stopped on the far side of the square and watched as the three kids rejoined the other five. He noticed as they all looked at the center orb. Miles nodded in comprehension. "Y'all are just waitin' to get your hands on that bad boy, aren't you?"

The girl holding the last orb glanced at her companions and then tossed it over her shoulder, letting it hit harmlessly behind them. The cage snapped shut and buzzed and crackled on the stone pavement.

"That's what I thought," Miles said. He thought for a moment on what he could do with his last orb. He knew no one could touch the center orb until his was detonated.

Swiftly, a ninja star came flying at his head. He ducked just in time as the star sank into the wood of the Giant Swing with a thud. "Oh hell," Miles panicked. He looked back at the silvery star embedded in the old red wood. "Have you no respect for this old thing, huh?"

He had to think fast, and move faster. He took off on his gliders as fast as he could. He weaved and ducked every which way. Metallic razors came flying all around him like bullets. He sighed with relief as each one clanged off the ground or off benches or posts. Each split second he kept expecting one to bury itself in his arms, chest, legs, or even worse, his head. He had to think of a way to use his last orb. He raced to the far side of the square again. He saw Gigi from the corner of his eye still standing in the same place with her arms behind her back.

"Enjoying the show so far?" Miles quipped as he zipped past her. "How about some bright ideas, Miss 'I don't belong here'." He circled back and forth still dodging ninja stars.

Gigi finally broke her silence. "They are testing you, Miles."

"Ah, cut the crap will ya? They are trying to *kill* me damnit."

"Use the orb, Miles," she instructed. "Just as you were before."

Miles whirled around and thought quickly about what she was saying. He held the orb in front of him. It was still glowing gold and emerald. He could feel the electric power that it carried within. It tingled his hands as he held it. *It can repel objects?* he thought to himself. He decided to test his theory. Another star came slicing through the air straight at him. He held the orb out to deflect it. The star clanged off the orb and cut his hand and finger in the process. "*Ah,*" Miles yelled. "That didn't work. It doesn't repel jack."

He forgot about his bleeding hand and took off again.

Think. Think Miles. His mind raced as he skated for his life. As the stars kept flying by, he finally realized it was not the smaller orb she was referring to, it was the center orb! He had to get his hands on it first. Then he thought of a plan.

He circled the edges of the square and behind the Giant Swing. Razor stars thumped into the ancient wood one after the other as he raced behind it. Expecting Miles to reappear on the other side of the stone pedestal, the kids were surprised that he had disappeared. The whole group of them stopped together. Suddenly, Miles came flying over their heads as he ramped off the pedestal of the Giant Swing. He tossed the final orb straight over his head as he flew over them. He landed just feet from the center orb and as soon as he landed the smaller orb zipped to the ground and exploded between him and the kids. They pulled back against the force of the detonation. Angrily, all eight of them tossed razor sharp stars directly at him. Miles skidded and turned as he barreled into the center orb. Instantly the orb flashed into a huge sphere of brilliant light, encasing Miles inside. All the razor stars stopped in mid-air, as if blocked by an invisible cushion, before they could penetrate the giant sphere. Miles stood defiantly and safely inside, smiling as the stars fell to the ground one by one. The angry attackers circled around him and tossed more stars at him, but only in futility.

Soon, the huge sphere began to crackle and pop. The energy shield was fading very quickly. Before he knew it, his protection was gone. He did not move though. He was finally trapped. They glided slowly towards him, forming a half-circle. All of them held the razor-sharp stars in their hands, ready to strike.

Then something happened that took Miles by complete surprise. The faces on the kids turned fearful. He noticed that they were looking past him and above his head. He turned around to see what made them so terrified. High at the top of one of the leg supports of the Giant Swing stood a masked figure, dressed all in black with a long flowing black cape. Her long, silky black hair cascaded down her shoulders and the shimmering black cape swirled in the wind. The figure glared at the kids below. Miles' eyes grew wide as he stared at the mysterious woman. On her upper arm was a single tattoo symbol of infinity. She was tall and lean and the mask she wore just covered her eyes. She stared at Miles' attackers with a commanding and firm look.

The terrified kids began to whisper the word, "*Wiyyân*," over and over.

"What the...?" was all Miles could say.

He turned back around to see the frightened kids swivel around and scatter quickly in all directions and disappear down the streets. Miles was stunned. He shook his head in amazement. He could not believe they all left just like that.

"Lady," Miles panted, catching his breath, "I don't know if you're their mother or what, but you sure scared the hell outta them!" Miles watched as the last kid disappeared. "How did you get way up…" Miles turned to look at the masked woman again but she was gone.

Chapter 3
The Bishops

Gigi and Miles slowly walked across the square until they stood before one another.

"What just happened here? Who was that?" Miles asked befuddled.

Gigi stared at him with a look of indifference. "Who was what?" was her reply.

"That lady up on the...didn't you see that?" Miles' voice rose. "Those punks were scared out of their wits and scattered like the wind! I'm sure glad, too. That was getting ridiculous out there."

Suddenly, Gigi's image beamed directly into Miles' CommVice on his wrist. Only her face appeared on the small screen. "You proved yourself victorious over the pawns. They left because you defeated them, Miles."

"The *pawns*?" Miles asked. "What is that? Some kind of gang name or something?"

"You must prepare for the next challenge however," Gigi continued, ignoring his question. "You have depleted a great deal of your energy."

"Yeah, no sh…Whoa wait! Next challenge? What are you talking about?" Miles began to panic. He did not like where this was going. "I don't want any more challenges. Besides, they were just some street punks giving me a bad first impression of this place. I just wanta go home!" He tried to reason with the face on his wrist. "Look, you said I don't belong here. So, I know you know something. Can't you just tell me how to get outta here?"

To his chagrin, Gigi remained silent. He looked all around the empty square for a street sign with directions or a perhaps a taxi. He saw nothing though. On the ground, he saw one of the metallic stars reflecting in the street lights. He picked it up and studied the razor-sharp weapon. Etched on one side was the chess symbol of a pawn. He stared at it curiously. "They left so quickly, they didn't even take their weapons with them," he muttered. "Geez."

He began to walk back to the area where the sign was that described the temple and the Great Swing, but as he walked, he was instantly teleported away.

Miles whirled around in a helpless panic. He found himself in a dark forest. His clothes had changed as well. He was now wearing some faded and badly worn clothes. They were drab brown pants and a dark green button down shirt. They looked like something from a refugee camp. He stood in the midst of a thickly wooded area. No leaves were on the trees and he could see his breath in the crisp night air. The sky was full of stars and a bright full moon. All he could hear was the sound of chirping frogs and crickets.

"Oh no, not another place," he panicked. "What...what is this place? Where am I now?" He looked down at his wrist but the CommVice was gone. His long sleeves nearly covered his hands. The shirt was at least two sizes too big for him. "Gigi?" he called out. He heard no answer. He saw nothing but the spindly leafless limbs of the trees as they shone in the moonlight. "I've had enough, OK? I want to go back now, please. I want to go back to my time, back to New Orleans."

"All in time, Miles," he heard a voice say from the darkness within the trees. Gigi emerged in full form from the thick trees and stood in the clearing alongside Miles. He looked at her peculiarly. She did not appear to look the same this time. There was something different about her. Something more... natural and more mature.

"Gigi?" Miles asked just to be sure. "Is that you?"
"Of course it is, Miles."
"You um...you look different. Your hair. Your hair is a lot

longer. And your face. It looks...I don't know." Miles scrambled for the right words to choose. He knew she was a hologram but suddenly he did not feel like saying something that offended her. It was a strange feeling. Why would a hologram be offended? "Your face seems more...sophisticated."

"You mean older?" Gigi asked with a smile.

Miles did his best to backtrack. "Oh *no*. I mean more like a fine wine that's aged. I mean, ripened. I mean, oh crap. I mean, I'll stop there." He was clearly embarrassed.

Gigi smiled even broader. "I understand, Miles."

He tried to change the subject. "What is this place? What are we doing here?" He looked down at his old clothing. "And why am I dressed like this?"

"You need time to rest," Gigi answered directly. "They will soon come looking for you again. You must prepare."

"What? The pawn gang again? No thank you. I'm steerin' clear of those little twerps. Why can't I go back to my own place in time right now?"

"No, the bishops will be looking for you next," she informed him. "And they won't be as kind, I'm afraid."

"Bishops?" Miles was clearly confused. "You mean like the head honcho of a diocese? A bishop wants to come after me? Hey, I'd like to think of myself as a good Catholic, so I don't think I'm going to be duking it out with some bishop. I think they frown on that."

"Not in the modern traditional sense, Miles," Gigi explained. "In the ancient world, bishops were not only members of the ecclesiastic but also defenders of the throne, and in most cases extremely cunning hunters."

Miles was perplexed. "Defenders of the throne?" It began to make sense to him. "Wait a sec. First there were pawns, and now you say bishops are next. You mean...like a game of *chess*?"

"Precisely."

"You mean to tell me this is all some sort of game?" Miles felt like his head was about to explode.

"But not necessarily a game, Miles. There are no inanimate pieces on a chess board. This is real. The challenge is real and the threat is real."

"But why?" Miles demanded. "Who wants to challenge me like this?" Miles stepped closer to Gigi. "Please. Tell me. Why were the pawns after me? Why were they trying to kill me?"

"They were not intending to kill you, Miles," Gigi answered. "They were testing you for your skill and feats of strength. You are here now. So, it is obvious that you passed."

"Why are we here in the woods?"

"You needed a place that you were accustomed to, so you could renew your spirit." Gigi reached out and placed her hand on his shoulder. She gazed at him as if she were a real person instead of a hologram.

Instinctively, Miles raised his hand and placed it on hers. He was stunned when he could actually feel the texture of her hand! He jumped back in surprise. "Hey! You're…you're real?" Gigi only looked back at him with a warm gaze. Miles slowly lifted his hand and caressed the side of her face. "You *are* real!" he whispered. "Why are you so familiar to me? Who *are* you?"

"Rest now, Miles. Soon it will be time."

Miles awoke from a deep slumber. The blankets pulled up to his chin were nice and cozy. He felt someone stir beside him. He could smell the familiar scent of his wife. It always intoxicated him. A feeling of sheer relief came over him when he realized Vicky was lying next to him in the warm bed. He looked around the dimly lit room and saw that it was a cabin. The walls were all wooden logs perfectly arranged and finely polished. He looked at the walls and the large room curiously. A small fireplace was across the room and was still smoldering. He sensed they must be in a cabin in the mountains. *Were they on vacation somewhere?* he wondered.

"Hey, you," he heard her sweet voice say.

He rolled over to see Vicky's beaming, smiling face. Relief washed over him once again. "Oh. I'm *so* glad to see you…" He kissed her passionately.

She sighed heavily and caressed his forehead. "Mmm, honey. Why aren't you like this every morning? I love it."

"I had the weirdest dream. You would not believe me even if I told you." She smiled at him. She loved to hear him tell her his dreams. He propped himself up on his elbow and looked around the room once again. "You're such a sly little devil. Where have you brought me this time? I love this cabin, baby."

She snickered softly. "Silly, you were the one that brought *me* here. You told me you needed to rest." Miles looked at her confused.

He began to remember what Gigi had been telling him in the forest. "Well yeah. I mean…wait. I thought she, I mean you…wait a minute. That bunch of kids were all after…Baby, where are our kids?" He began to panic.

She put her finger to his lips. "Shhh. You still need to rest, my love. Just focus on me. I'm here to calm you. Rest with me, my dearest one. You will need your strength. Soon it will be time again."

"I don't understand. I just want to be here with you. I only want to be with you."

"Shhh," she whispered again. She kissed him lightly as he closed his eyes and drifted off to sleep once more.

Miles startled awake. He found himself sitting on the ground and propped up against a large tree. He was still in the woods and the air was much cooler than before. He looked around but Gigi was nowhere to be seen. He had no idea how long he had been asleep. Could it have been hours, or maybe just minutes? He looked up at the sky to see how much the moon had moved, but it was no longer visible. Neither were the stars.

He got to his feet and called out, "Gigi?" There was no answer. "Vicky?" For a brief moment, he had hopes that she would appear again. Even the frogs and crickets had gone silent. His instincts became very aware. He sensed something around him. Or perhaps something near. It was all too quiet for his taste. It was not long before his instincts proved true. An arrow came slicing through the cold night air and made a *thunk* on the tree next to him. *They missed on purpose*, Miles thought. *That was a warning shot.* "Don't have to tell me twice," Miles said out loud.

With that, he took off running through the thick woods. He ran as fast as he could in the opposite direction from where the arrow came. He heard yelling echo through the forest. There were many voices. It was as if a whole throng of hunters were after him. They were shouting in a language he did not understand. Then there was gunfire. Miles ducked as he ran as if he could dodge bullets. He knew it was almost fruitless to do so, but he did it anyway. There were long moments in between shots and the shouting grew angrier in tone as the hunt continued.

Miles ducked behind a tree to hide and catch his breath.

He tried to listen to see which direction the voices and gunshots were heading. Were they still on his tail? Another shot rang out. He listened and waited but did not hear a sound of a bullet hitting a branch or tree trunk. *Those sound like really old rifles*, he thought to himself. *What the hell are they using?*

The voices grew louder. They were getting closer to him. Another shot rang out and a bullet glanced off a tree just to the left of him. He took off running again. He heard the men shouting and giving orders in their frantic chase. Miles was able to pick out a few of the words as they shouted. "*Posle nikh!*" they shouted over and over.

Miles listened to the accent and tone and the fierce command of the voice. "That sounds like Russian! Geez, man. What the hell..." Miles mumbled to himself as he ran.

He emerged from the woods and ran into a clearing. The moon was still behind the clouds, but it was still bright enough that he could see where he was running. He soon realized he was on a hillside overlooking what appeared to be a large city. However, it did not look anything like the futuristic Bangkok. He could see a large river running through the valley below amidst a city that looked as if it were in ruin or total devastation. There were dim lights scattered about the rubble of the city, but none of which seemed like electrical lights. They all appeared to be firelight. "Where the hell am I?"

The shouts came out of the clearing as well and the shots

sounded louder than ever. "After them," he heard them shout.

Miles looked over his shoulder to see a group of soldiers dressed in gray uniforms and gray and red caps. They were running after him carrying weapons of all kinds, not just rifles. They had bows and arrows, muskets and crossbows, and even swords. "That was in English," he shouted. He ran as hard as he could. Just before he reached the other side of the clearing and re-entered the woods…he disappeared.

Miles stood atop a tremendous skyscraper. It was so high it was as if he were looking down from an airplane. He was in the Bangkok of the future again. He instantly recognized the gravity glider vehicles zipping every which way around the city and buildings below. His hands trembled. His mind ached from the constant change from so much teleportation. He panted as he tried to catch his breath. His tattered clothes were gone. He was dressed in the same dark body suit that he had worn before. He looked around the roof of the building nervously, still half-expecting an angry mob of Russians chasing him, but he was all alone. He looked down at his wrist and his CommVice was there, but the screen was blank.

He lifted it and spoke into the device, "Gigi, you out there?" There was no reply. All he could here were the sounds of the city below. And a very faint buzzing sound. He could not tell what it was or where it was coming from.

He looked across the cityscape and noticed a large digital

clock atop one of the many skyscrapers. It read 2:04 A.M. Miles nodded in acceptance. "At least I got a *little* sleep." Again, he could hear the faint buzzing noise over the sound of the city traffic below. "Man, that is weird."

He stepped to the edge of the roof and looked straight down. He had no idea how high the building was, but he had never been on the roof of one even close to being this tall. "*Ay carumba*," he shouted, trying to channel his best imitation of Bart Simpson. He had been on top of the Empire State Building once when he was a teen but this one made that building look like a toy.

He looked around the roof and in the sky above to try and detect the sound of the buzzing. He looked back down the side of the building once more when suddenly a flying craft came zipping straight up at him from below. Miles jumped back just in time as the strange looking aircraft soared high above his head. It was a round, flying sphere that was transparent and looked very much like the center orb before it had detonated. Yet this one was zipping around in all directions as if it were defying every law of physics. In the center of the machine was a man clad in black just like the pawns, except the stripe running down his suit was dazzling silver.

Suddenly, another sphere came buzzing over the edge of the roof and took dead aim at Miles. He hit the deck as soon as the aircraft whizzed over him. The man inside was identical to the other, dressed in jet black with a streak of gold running along his sides. Both spheres sparkled with glowing colors as they flew in majestic aerials around the top of the building.

"I guess you're the guys I've been waitin' on, huh?" Miles shouted.

"The Bishops," Gigi answered. She appeared on the screen of his CommVice.

"Well how the hell do I fight 'em? I'm just a sittin' duck up here!"

"Move faster!" she instructed.

"Well, *duh!!*" Miles kept low to the roof's surface and an eye on the swirling spheres. "What the hell are they flying in?"

Without hesitation, and as if it should be obvious, Gigi replied, "Sphere Chasers. You must learn them quickly."

Miles ducked behind an air vent as one of the chasers buzzed just over his head. "Sphere Chasers? What's the deal with floating balls around here anyway? I feel like I'm being attacked by a cheesy screensaver! What's next? Flying toasters?" The second chaser slammed to the roof of the building and began rolling towards him. The sphere tumbled while the pilot remained steady inside in a dazzling display of light and sparks. Miles had no choice but to make a run for it. He dove behind another ventilation shaft in the nick of time as the chaser raced past. "Gigi, how do I fight these guys?"

From the corner of his eye, a third sphere instantly appeared on the far side of the roof. The luminescent bars of the sphere flashed simultaneously and formed the sphere from inside out in a manner of microseconds. Miles was stunned at how it appeared from nowhere. He opened his mouth. "Holy…" was the only word his lips could utter. A few of the glowing bars disappeared momentarily as if to make an opening.

"You must learn quickly," Gigi repeated. "Go *now*."

Both of his pursuers were high above the roof and preparing to attack in unison. Miles darted towards his awaiting vessel, not knowing how to maneuver it once he got inside. Both Sphere Chasers were right on top of him as he dove like a football player hurtling himself towards the goal line. He flew head first into the glowing sphere. Instantly the bars closed the portal and Miles tumbled to the bottom of the glowing orb. His momentum sent the sphere sailing over the edge of the roof. Miles yelped as he saw the roof disappear from beneath him, only to be replaced by the city lights far below. The sphere began to fall towards the Earth in a brilliant ball of glittering light. The other two chasers were zipping straight down towards him in an equally fascinating flash.

"Oh crap," Miles yelled. He looked all around the insides of the craft as it fell. It was virtually empty. All he could see was what appeared to be two shimmering metallic plates at the bottom. He could not see how someone was supposed to control such a thing. He could see the reflection of his sphere in the windows of the buildings that surrounded him as he continued to fall. He could see the other two chasers were still right on top of him. Passengers in gravity gliders raced up and down the sides of the same building, watching the aerial show next to them in awe. One little boy riding with his mother was going down at the same pace as Miles was falling. The boy's eyes widened in disbelief. Miles could hardly believe it himself. Miles managed to give the little boy a smile as he fell. The boy smiled back and giggled. Even though he was hurtling straight down the side of a building inside a glowing sphere, Miles' parental instincts kicked in. "What are you doing out so late?" he yelled out to the boy. "You should be in bed!"

One sphere swooped down below him and then circled back up and slammed into his, breaking his fall and sending his sphere sailing to the right. The little boy laughed and waved to Miles, saying, "Bye!" As soon as Miles started to fall again, the other sphere came up from below and bounced him towards the sky. Miles was helpless as he tumbled around inside the craft like laundry in a dryer.

"Gigi, how do I control this damn thing? They're playin' ping pong with me."

"Put your feet on the plates," she finally commanded. "Learn faster, Miles."

As he tossed about, he darted his eyes around trying to

find the metallic plates. They were right above his face. He tried to maneuver around while the ball spun in the air as it continued to fall. He saw his two attackers coming after him again. The objects and gliders on the streets below were getting bigger by the second. If he did not get his feet on those plates quickly, his sphere would soon come crashing down to Earth. He managed to swing his feet around. The force of the fall made it difficult for him to thrust himself towards the plates, but he pushed as hard he could. In a split second before the two chasers both crashed into him, Miles flung his body towards the plates and his feet landed squarely on them. Instantly his feet were locked into place. A cushioned back support encased his body and two handles appeared for him to grab hold of. Immediately the craft began to slow its fall and began to float horizontally. The two chasers narrowly missed him as he darted to the side.

"Oh man, this is *wild*." Miles shouted. "Thank God it stopped. Now I know what laundry feels like." He tried to move the handles but they would not budge. He was securely positioned in the sphere now, but he could not figure out the controls. He continued to float sideways and was getting dangerously close to one of the buildings. He began to panic as he was getting closer and closer to the building. "I can't control this thing." Instinctively he turned his body, as if to run the other way even though his feet were secure in place. Suddenly the sphere turned in the way that Miles had, narrowly missing the glass of the building. He soon realized his body movement was the key. He shifted his weight on his feet to the right; the sphere turned right. He shifted the other way, and the sphere turned left. He moved his hands upward on the handles, and it went up. Miles was getting the hang of it in a hurry. "Oh, this is *sweet*."

"Yes, Miles," Gigi said from his CommVice approvingly. "You learned quickly."

"Yeah, yeah, thanks," he answered sarcastically. "You're not the one dizzy as hell."

He did indeed learn quickly. Immediately Miles got the feel of the ingenious flying machine. He maneuvered it with ease and evaded every pass by his chasers with nifty turns and spins that seemed to defy the laws of physics and gravity. No matter which way he moved, he remained upright. The sphere moved around him. He eventually got the upper hand on the other two and began bouncing them off one another as if they had become the ping pong balls.

"How do you like that, *pal?*" Miles yelled out to them as he swiftly banged into the other spheres. Miles soared over the vast lighted city and laughed as his foes futilely chased him. "Ha ha, this is *amazing*." He felt the adrenaline rush through him as he shot across the night sky above the sparkling buildings and highways below. The spheres dazzled the night sky in an aerial-acrobatics show. Even though he knew he was still being hastily pursued, Miles was beginning to enjoy the chase.

The view of Bangkok was breathtaking. The enormity of it all was awe-inspiring. The bright, hypnotizing Bangkok of the future set against the backdrop of the darkened sea was amazing to Miles. As he sliced through the air, keeping one eye on the others and one on the city below, he smiled and said to himself, "I can't believe I'm doing this. I wish Vicky were here."

Suddenly one of the other men got the better of him and slammed into his sphere. He went careening out of control high above the city. Sparks flew as if an enormous firework had gone off, and Miles was in the center of it. "Ah, you little *rat*," Miles yelled. He quickly regained control and decided to fly to a lower altitude. He reached the tops of the skyscrapers again and began to use the network of high-rises as an obstacle course to keep the others at bay. The three flyers raced and turned in and around the intricate network of glassed buildings. It was a cat and mouse chase like Miles had never been a part of before.

"Miles," Gigi warned, "You must take care not to bounce off the glass. The sphere chaser will not have the effect you are thinking of."

"Oh, you know what I'm thinking now?" Miles fired back matter-of-factly.

Gigi ignored the question. "It will not bounce. If you strike the buildings, the glass will eliminate the sphere's power and you will fall to the *ground*. I advise you to get out of here."

"Oh, *now* you tell me," Just then he was slammed again. He narrowly missed the edge of a building but quickly regained control. Both the other chasers were clearly getting the upper hand on him in the confined flying space. They rammed into him again and again, bouncing him around between the tall skyscrapers like a fiery tennis ball. Miles did everything he could to keep his sphere from careening into one of the buildings.

"You *must* get out of here," Gigi insisted.

"I know. I *know*." Miles shifted his weight and raised his hands as forcefully as he could so the chaser would shoot straight up. As the sphere began to rise, raindrops began to hit his face. He could not tell if it was his sweat pouring off his hair, or if it was actually starting to rain. "What is that? Rain?"

"Affirmative. That's not good," she answered.

Miles glanced down at his wrist. "Why is that not good?"

"You must find a place to land immediately," she insisted.

"*Why* is that not good?" he shouted louder. Sparks began to fly as each drop of rain hit the sphere chaser. Miles could feel the control of the aircraft begin to diminish. It was not responding as well to his weight and directional maneuvers. "Uh, Gigi. I take it these things aren't waterproof."

"Correct. The power cells harness the rays of the sun and can sustain that power even at night."

"You mean like solar cells?" he asked.

"No. Electromagnetic radiation cells. The only problem is they are severely weakened by water. You must land immediately."

"I'm trying!" He tried his best to steer the chaser to either the ground or try for the roof of a building.

"Not the rooftops. You may undershoot and hit the windows." she warned him. "We *must* land on the ground."

The other two chasers were right behind him, and they were sparking in the rain just like Miles' was. The three descended rapidly as the rain intensified. Miles spotted an alley in between two shorter buildings and did his best to direct his sphere towards it. One sphere was still behind him. The other lost control and went careening down another alleyway and smashed to the pavement. The flyer inside was sent rolling and tumbling into a wall.

Miles tried to ease up but it was no use. His sphere came crashing through the alley and into the standing water drenching it. He went barreling into some trash bins, and with that the sphere chaser disappeared in a brilliant flash of light. He sat up in the pile of trash bins. Rubbish was strewn everywhere. As soon as he looked up, the other sphere came barreling towards his head, crackling and sparking as he ducked out of the way.

The man inside went sailing through the standing, trash-covered water. His dark glasses were flung from his face. Miles staggered to his feet while the rain poured down. Coughing and panting for air, he strained to see through the rain. He wanted to make sure the other man was alright. Miles found him several yards away, still lying in a heap on the wet pavement.

"Hey buddy, you alright?" Miles shouted over the thundering rain.

The young man finally moved. He moaned as if he were in pain. He sat up and saw Miles standing over him. He was a young man, no more than eighteen or nineteen.

Miles looked on in disbelief. "Why, you're just a high school kid! Dude, you OK? I think both you guys landed a lot harder than I did."

As the rain fell harder, the young man smiled at Miles and said in Thai, "*Mạn pĕn keīyrti khrạb.*"

Miles could not understand. "I'm sorry?" He reached his hand out to the young man. He helped him get to his feet.

"*Mạn pĕn keīyrti,*" he said again, smiling and shaking Miles' hand.

Still not understanding, Miles replied, "Well...yeah. You're welcome."

At that moment they heard a yell from the other end of the alley. It was a yell of defiance and of war. The other man had found them and was yelling over the pouring rain. The young man immediately released Miles' hand and backed away with fear in his eyes. The yelling man produced, as if from nowhere, a long glowing sword. He began to charge towards them, yelling and screaming. The young man had no other choice but to draw his glowing sword as well and began to yell in the same fashion.

"Oh crap," Miles belched. "I guess this mean's timeout is over?" He took off running down the alley in the other direction as the two young men chased after him brandishing their glowing weapons.

He ran as hard as he could even though he was already out of breath from the harrowing crash. He dashed down one alleyway and then another, but he could not lose them. He jumped over walls, over fences, and tried doors but found them all to be locked. He headed down another path as the rain fell down his face, his shoes splashing the water with every step. Soon, he was trapped against a wall. There was no other way to turn. The wall was too high to climb. He looked around in a panic, trying to find something to use as a weapon. All that was there was an old beat-up trashcan. He grabbed the lid and used it as a shield.

The two men came sliding to a stop, still holding their glowing weapons. They knew they had him trapped. Both were wearing their darkened shades again. They slowly advanced towards him.

"Haven't you guys had enough?" Miles pleaded with them.

At that moment, they both charged at him at top speed, yelling and screaming with their swords pointed right at him. Miles braced himself and held the trash lid in front of him, preparing for the collision.

Suddenly, the men came skidding to a halt. Their swords disappeared. They stood frozen only feet away from Miles in stunned silence. They looked above Miles' head and removed their dark shades from their eyes. The young man who had spoken to Miles earlier had a look of terror on his face. He wiped the rain from his eyes but could not speak. Miles whirled around to see the woman in the mask and cape again, perched high upon the wall and glaring through the rain at the two men.

"*Wiyyân*," one of the men hissed."

"*You*," Miles exclaimed in amazement.

The two young men went running away as fast as they could into the rain. Miles looked away just for an instant to see them flee. He turned around and asked, "Who are…?" But she was gone again. Miles stood dumbfounded in the dead-end alley.

Chapter 4
The Knight

Miles sloshed his way down the alley, trying to find his way out. He realized he was still carrying the trash lid and he tossed it aside against a wall. The masked woman in the cape had left him speechless, and he soon started to feel some pain in his leg from the crash in the sphere chaser. He began to limp as he searched for a way out of the alleys and into the open streets.

He looked down at his CommVice but the screen was blank. "Gigi?" he said into it, but there was no answer. "Of course," he mumbled.

He was dead tired from the running and being chased. The rain fell harder as he walked. His clothes were soaked through. Looking around, he tried to see if any of the buildings in the distance seemed familiar. None of them did however, yet he was still fascinated with his new surroundings. Despite having mastered the gravity gliders and sphere chasers, he still could not believe he was actually here. It was as if he were in a real-life video game. He could not help but think of his family though and why he was here. It was one of the few moments he had to contemplate his situation.

He found a stack of wet wooden planks that looked good enough to rest on. They were under a small awning and out of the rain. He decided to take a rest on them. He sat down and wiped the rain from his face. "Boy, I am beat," he said to himself.

"You think you beat, huh?" asked a voice on the other side of the stack of wood.

Miles jolted upright. He had not noticed the man before he sat down. Sitting on a small chair with a plate of food on his lap was an old man that appeared to be homeless. He wore a tattered hat and brown coat and had on old rubber boots. He was of African descent.

"I'm sorry, I didn't see you there," Miles said.

"You think you beat, huh?" the man said again. "Man's gotta know his limitations."

Miles recognized his accent right away. "You're American."

"That be right, my friend," the man smiled happily. "From New Orleans, to be exact."

"Really?" Miles asked excitedly. "Me, too." He was curious though. This man was not the first American he had noticed in the Bangkok of the future. "How did you get to be way over here in Thailand?"

The man answered matter-of-factly, "Came over in the Great Migration in the twenties." He motioned to the food on his plate. "You hungry? I can cook you up some of this if you want."

Miles looked at the food on the plate. It did not look too appetizing. "No offense, but what the hell is that?"

"It's alley rat."

Miles tried not to lose what little food was left in his belly. "How the hell can you eat alley rat?"

The man sat up in his chair. It seemed it was a question he was more than happy to answer. "Well, you just don't slap your alley rat on a plate and say here it is! First you gotta gut it, cut the head and the tail off, claws and what-not." Miles winced at the thought. "Then you cook it in a pan and sauté it in some wine sauce. If you got any wine. It's good eatin' if you want some."

"No thanks," Miles answered.

The man leaned forward, still insisting. "You sure? It ain't no trouble. I can cook you up some right now."

"No, I'm good. Thanks." Miles sat on the wood and rested and watched it rain. He thought about what the man had said about migrating. "The Great Migration? What's that all about?

Why are there so many Americans here?"

"You mean you don't know?" the man laughed. "'Cause the U.S. got taken over, that's why." Miles glanced over at him as if he were a madman. "Early part of the century the government was so soft and politically correct on illegals that soon they overrun the place. Not just from Latin countries or Europe neither, but from everywhere. They poured in from countries from every corner of Asia and the Middle East. It's like the world's cultures flipped from one side to the other." The man chuckled to himself. "Politically correct. They see where that got 'em." He stuffed some food into his mouth. He continued with his mouth full. "Those of us that could got out or got pushed out. By the time they got control of the borders again, it was too late. Just like that, the U.S. I used to know was gone. Sad in a way." The old man seemed to be reminiscing about former times and pondered them for a moment. Then he picked up some more alley rat and shoved it into his mouth. "Anyway, not so bad over here. I kinda like it."

"It was gone? Pushed out?" Miles asked dumbfounded. "You're kidding me."

"Nope."

"That's unbelievable. We just lost our country? That's insane." He immediately started thinking about his children. Even in 2005 he could not imagine seeing such an event occurring in the U.S. What would happen to his children? He began to feel ashamed for what might happen in the present in his country. "That just doesn't sound right at all. And here. It doesn't seem you can catch a break here either. I haven't stopped running since I got here. I mean hell, what's the point?" Miles suddenly felt very depressed. His current predicament and the sobering news of his country's future left him shaken.

The old man began to laugh heartily. Miles looked at him as if he were nuts. "*What's the point* he asks! He riddles me!" Miles did not think it was too funny, though. The man sat up with a serious look on his face. "Did you ever see that old-timey cartoon where the bald eagle is flying through bullets and all sorts of hell, trying to get back to his little bald eagle babies?" Miles shook his head wearily. "And suddenly two X's come across his eyes and he says, 'So, what the hell? It ain't easy bein' an eagle!' And the bald eagle begins to fall down and down and then BAM! Just a splatter of feathers on the ground and the United States no longer has its national bird."

Miles looked at him as if he were crazier than ever. "No, I never saw that."

The man laughed as hard as he could and shouted, "Me neither!" Miles just shook his head and stared at the wet ground, still depressed. "No," the man became serious again, "The bald eagle's got too much self-respect. America ain't lost. We just gave up on her."

Miles refused to believe it. "No. That can't happen." The

old man gave him a sympathetic grin. Miles got to his feet and wiped his face again. He felt re-energized. "I think I am alright now. I better head out. Thanks for the company." The rain had lightened up so Miles headed on his way.

The old man watched him disappear down the street and muttered to himself, "No, you ain't beat yet, Devereaux. You ain't beat yet."

As he walked down the darkened, silent alleys, Miles slipped his fingers inside his collar and produced the amulet that hung around his neck. His fingers traced the initials on the back of the tarnished talisman. First the letter G, then the letter B. He turned it over as he walked to see the face of the young dark-haired girl behind the old, hazy glass. Why did she seem so familiar? He had almost forgotten it was hanging around his neck. He felt comforted that it was there while he went from one challenge to the next. He just did not know why.

The streets were quiet as he walked, but he could hear the faint sounds of activity somewhere in the vicinity. It almost sounded like another open-air market or a street fair. But then another sound could be heard. He could hear something that sounded eerily familiar echoing down the darkened alleys. It was eerie because he could not see it but also exciting at the same time. *What could it be?* he thought to himself. The sound came closer. It was either the low rumbling hum of an engine motor, or the low, sustained growl of a dragon. Whatever it was, Miles had a feeling it was most certainly meant to get his attention.

He stepped lighter as he approached each cross-way in the alley, hoping to stay on top of whatever sound was creeping around in the dark. Suddenly, a flash of light went zipping past down a cross-way behind him. He quickly whirled around to see what it was, but it was too late. His eyes widened as the hum of the motor became louder. "I know that sound..." he whispered to himself. He quickened his pace and walked as fast as he could towards the street noise he had heard before. Again, the rumbling motor echoed down the empty streets. With his ears trained to the sound, he followed it until he caught sight of a flash of brilliant red light. A rider went roaring past the cross-way just behind him. "*Whoa!*" he yelled. For a split-second he saw it and he knew exactly what it was. He did not know *who* it was, but there was no mistaking where the roar was coming from.

Somewhat excited but still frightened, he took off running as fast he could. He had to get out of the alleys and back to where some action was. He ran hard towards the sounds of the street activity just ahead. Soon he popped out onto a very crowded pedestrian street. There were lights and signs everywhere and he quickly noticed, even at this late hour, there were people *everywhere*. No wonder it sounded so much like a street fair to him.

There were food vendors, clothing stalls, and trinket sellers spread up and down the crowded street. People were walking everywhere, talking and laughing. None of them appeared to take notice that it was well after three in the morning. The smell of food wafted through the air and suddenly Miles felt hungrier than he had ever been before. He saw the many food booths selling all kinds of seafood, vegetables, and even fried selections; none of which came close to resembling alley rat. Amulet vendors were everywhere as well. Once again, he clasped his fingers around the silvery-tarnished amulet hanging around his neck as he strolled down the busy area. It was then he noticed he was back in his street clothes from earlier. "How the hell does that happen?" he muttered to himself.

He decided he wanted something to eat. He looked down at his CommVice and remembered it was also a means to purchase things. "May as well use it," he said. He perused many of the food vendors and found one that looked wonderful to him. On a grill, right on the street, a woman was cooking what appeared to be chicken kabobs along with seasoned grilled vegetables. Miles held up one finger to the woman and said in English, "One please." The woman happily gave him a nice long kabob covered with perfectly cooked chicken and sliced vegetables. He raised his CommVice and the woman quickly scanned it for his purchase. She smiled, saying thank you in her own language. He knew exactly what she was saying and he was all too happy to thank her. He was starving. "No. Thank *you*!"

The chicken turned out to be duck and it was delicious. "Oh man, I'm in Heaven," Miles drawled as he picked the kabob clean one bite at a time. The zucchini and squash and mushrooms were cooked and seasoned to perfection, as well was the grilled duck. He finished the last bite of duck and smiled happily. "Oh yeah…" Soon, he needed something to drink, but that was not a problem either. There were vendors for almost every kind of drink one could imagine. "A beer sounds good to me," he said, searching around for one who had some ice-cold brews. He found one right away and used his electronic device to buy a bottle of frosty beer. He gulped it down in a satisfying manner. "Ah!" he belched with a big smile on his face.

"Enjoying yourself?" a familiar voice asked. Gigi appeared from out of nowhere and stood with a slanted grin on her face. "I've never seen a duck kabob and a beer disappear so quickly."

Miles looked at her awkwardly. "I am now, thank you. I forgot sarcasm was one of your sub-routines." He wiped his mouth with his sleeve. "You get a little famished when you're being chased all over creation and crash to the street from a thousand feet. Where the hell you been anyway? Taking a nap or something?" She ignored him. They began walking together down the crowded street. "What is this place anyway?"

"Do you like it?" she asked.

"Yeah, reminds me of the French Quarter. These folks would probably feel right at home there."

"I'm glad you like it, Miles. This is Khao San Road," Gigi explained. "It is very popular with tourists and locals alike."

"I can see that," he replied. "It's true, this town never does sleep. Amazing."

"You handle yourself well, Miles," she continued. "You are to be commended for your adaptability and perseverance."

Miles was not in the mood. "Well, you can save the medal ceremony." He stopped walking and looked directly at Gigi. "Look, I've played your little game, I've tried the local cuisine and I've seen some really cool stuff, but can I just go home now? I mean, what's this all about? Can't you just level with me for once?"

"The game is not over yet, Miles," she answered directly.

"I was afraid you were going to say that," he deadpanned. "By the way, I think someone has been following me."

"You are correct."

"And I'm pretty sure he or she is riding a sports bike. A really freaking cool one," he added.

"Yes, we haven't much time."

"Listen, Gigi. I didn't ask to play this game. I didn't ask to be here in this time. But I am asking if you can please just let me go home?"

She placed her hand on his shoulder, "Miles, there are still many things yet to uncover. You must learn about yourself. Learning means growing. Growing leads to revelation, but growing also means patience; and in some cases, bravery. You would not have been chosen if you were not considered courageous. Come, I want to show you something."

"Chosen for what? Damnit!" Miles felt himself being pulled even though he was not moving. "Now what do you want to show…?"

Suddenly he found himself standing in front of a grand palace. Gone were the crowds and street vendors. It was just him and Gigi standing at the bottom of a large staircase that led to a white stone palace adorned with golden precipices and spires that reached high into the night sky.

"Wow," Miles exclaimed. "What's this place?"

"It is called Wat Traimit. It is the Temple of the Golden Buddha."

He was curious. "Golden Buddha, huh? Okay, what about it?"

"It is a large statue made of solid gold."

"Yeah, okay. I guess that sounds pretty cool. Can we see it?"

Without warning, they were zapped from outside the temple and suddenly were standing inside the chapel before the enormous statue of the Golden Buddha.

"*Geez,*" Miles gasped. "How do you *do* that?" He soon caught sight of the enormous golden statue of the seated Buddha. He shook his head. "I can't get used to all this zipping around. It's making me dizzy." He stared at the large statue but soon felt uneasy about being in such a place so late at night. "Are you sure we can be in here?" He hesitated for a moment, and then walked closer to it. "This is incredible! I've never seen anything like it."

Gigi began to explain the statue as if she were a tour guide. "The Golden Buddha is believed to have been cast from gold as far back as the thirteenth century. It is made of nearly eighty-three percent pure gold, and stands over four meters high, and weighs over five tons."

"Five tons? Holy cow," Miles blurted out.

"However," she continued, "Its true history was not discovered until just over a hundred years ago, in 1955." Miles was still struck by such a palpable statement regarding the year. "Sometime over the centuries, the statue was covered over in plaster to disguise it from thieves and looters. It stayed that way, unbeknownst to the public, until men were attempting to move it to Wat Traimit in 1955. However, the statue was so heavy it broke the ropes and came crashing to the ground, cracking the plaster. The workers discovered that the statue was not made of plaster at all. The cracked plaster revealed that it was actually made of pure gold."

"Incredible!" Miles said again.

"Since the secret was revealed so close to the commemoration of the twenty-fifth Buddhist Era, many people of Thailand believed the discovery to be miraculous."

"What does that mean? The twenty-fifth Buddhist Era?" he asked.

"It means that it's been 2500 years since the passing of Gautama Buddha," she answered.

"You mean *the* Buddha himself?"

"Precisely." Gigi walked closer to the statue and stood next to Miles. "You see Miles; you never know what something may be until you look closer underneath. If you peel back the layers, you find that there is something more to be revealed."

Miles tilted his head and looked at her for a moment. "Just what exactly are you trying to say?"

"I'm saying it's time to go. The knight awaits."

Suddenly they were standing outside again in front of the temple. Miles was no longer in his street clothes; instead he was dressed in his jet-black body suit with majestic purple stripe along the sides. It startled him yet again.

Then he noticed something across the way. He was stunned to see an incredible looking sports motorcycle. His eyes widened and he smiled with a glint of delight.

"Now *this* I know how to drive!" Standing in the darkness

was a sleek, black sport motorcycle with a matching majestic purple stripe racing down the sides. It was truly an engineering marvel on two wheels. Being a long-time motorcycle driver and expert on everything and anything that had to do with them, Miles knew exactly what it was. "The Ferrari V4 sports cycle. Aerodynamic in the most precise layouts ever conceived. A concept bike in my day that could be equipped with the V12 technology engine and reach speeds of over 300 miles per hour." He walked around the magnificent motorcycle step by step. "But no longer a concept, I see." He smiled broadly at it. "Very sweet *indeed*."

In the distance, he could hear the sound of an engine revving. Miles instantly knew it must be the sound of another V4. At the crest of a hill in the distance the rider revealed himself. Sitting upon a replica of the same bike that stood next to Miles was the knight. His motorcycle was fire-blazing red and he was dressed in an equally fire-blazing red body suit and helmet. His shield on the helmet was darkened over. The engine roared over and over again.

Miles stared at the rider in disbelief. "You gotta be kidding me," he said under his breath. He stood and yelled at the rider defiantly. "You wanna ride with me, do ya? Huh? Only if you're man enough." Miles' confidence was sky-high. If there was one thing he knew how to ride, it was motorcycles, and he was all too happy to try this hog out. He straddled the sleek-black V4 and donned his helmet. He flipped up the visor and looked over at Gigi. She was no longer there. Miles was perplexed, but then he looked at his CommVice. She appeared on the tiny screen. "He wants to mess with me? He's got it."

"Careful of the bravado, Miles," she warned.

At the top of the hill, tires screeched and spun with a trail of smoke behind as the red rider came flying down the hill directly at Miles.

"You're in *my* wheelhouse now, son!" Miles called out. He flipped his visor down and switched on the engine. It roared to life. Within seconds he was racing straight at the red rider in a blaze of black and purple. He came closer and closer to the knight and at the last second, the knight went sailing to the right and went ramping over several park benches. Miles kept going straight as an arrow, never once flinching at the first charge.

Gigi's eyes widened. Even she was in disbelief. Miles was more than up to challenge. He raced over the crest of the hill and disappeared. The red knight went speeding after him.

Miles raced through the nighttime streets of Bangkok with his head down, swerving in between and around gliders. The red racer matched his every move, staying right on his tail. Gigi appeared on Miles' CommVice again as he continued to race through the city.

"Miles, where are you going?" she asked, sounding

slightly aghast.

"I don't know, but this dude ain't kiddin' around," he answered frankly. "I need to get him away from all these buildings and cars. Bikes like these only draw attention." He thought quickly as he maneuvered effortlessly through the futuristic landscape. He was like a pro riding the sleek sports racer. He knew he was in trouble with the other biker, but he was also loving the ride. "We need to draw him out somewhere. Somewhere out in the open, away from all this."

"Affirmative," Gigi answered. "Turn where I tell you to."

"Is he still back there?"

"Yes," she replied, "right on your ass!"

Miles had to laugh out loud even as he raced down the streets at incredible speed. "A hologram that says 'ass'. Ha ha! I love it."

"Slang is another of my subroutines. I felt it was appropriate. Do you not agree? Turn right here."

Miles skidded on the motorcycle as he quickly tried to turn right. "Oh *sonuvabitch. Turn,* you bastard." The bike roared and slid on the wet pavement and barely turned upright before racing down another road. The red rider made the same turn in sleek style and stayed right on Miles. "Yes. Very appropriate. You damn right Gigi ol' pal."

"Stay on this road," Gigi instructed, "Keep him at bay. We'll draw him out to an open area called Happy Land."

"Happy Land? Seriously?" Miles just shook his head.

"Yes. It's a seaside village and is also a wide-open space on the road to Chonburi."

"If you say so," Miles answered.

As they drew further away from the city, the road became more isolated and less traveled. Soon, they were the only drivers on the road. Miles sensed the red rider closing in on him so he hit the gas even harder, racing down the straight, darkened road. He had reached over 150km/hour when the red rider came inching closer to his back wheel. The glow of the city behind them kept a good light over them in the night sky. Sweat poured down Miles' face as he rode. He had to flip his visor up so he could see as the glass had begun to fog over. He swerved from side to side on the open road but he could not shake the steady red knight.

Suddenly, Miles heard him rev the engine hard. Without warning, the red knight produced a long glowing jousting spear from the side of his racer. It was at least fifteen feet long and glowed an icy blue color. It was tipped with a silver, razor-sharpened point.

"Holy crap," Miles yelled.

Just as he yelled, he ducked as the razor point went zipping over his head. The red racer undercut Miles on his left and Miles lost control. His motorcycle went sailing out from underneath him. Miles instinctively leapt from the bike just in time and went into a slide as if he were coming into home plate. Sparks flew as the motorcycle went skidding off the road and into the dirt. Miles finally came to a stop himself. He felt the burn of the pavement through his clothes, down his legs and side, but he knew right away he was not badly hurt.

Miles panted as he sat up and watched the red knight skid around to a stop hundreds of yards away. He could hear the engine of the V4 humming in the night. He watched as the rider sat with his spear glowing eerily in the distance.

"Where the hell did he get that?" Miles muttered out loud. "He *is* a knight. For *real!*" He shook nervously after his crash and dramatic slide on the pavement. His leg ached from the long burn it had taken, but he knew he could have been in much worse shape. "I don't know what these clothes are made of but thank God for whatever it is."

He looked over at his damaged motorcycle across the road lying on its side in the weeds and dirt. He tried to think of how the red knight could have produced such a weapon out of thin air. "He got it out of the bike?" He looked down at his CommVice but once again the screen was blank. "Of course. You're gone again."

Cautiously, Miles got to his feet. The red knight was far off, but not that far. Miles would have to make a run for it as fast he could towards his bike. He had no idea how much the V4 would weigh. Could he lift it back up by himself? If it were a Harley or anything like that he knew he could not lift it alone. Plus, he did not know how damaged it would be after the crash. Would it even run again?

Miles thought out loud once again. "It's my only chance. Here goes nothing." Keeping one eye on the glowing spear in the distance, Miles dashed towards his fallen motorcycle. Surprisingly the red knight never made a move. He sat quietly, holding his joust firmly in the night.

Miles got to the V4 lying in a heap. The purple streak down the side was badly scratched and some light smoke was coming from the rear, but the wheels seemed to be undamaged and the rest of the bike seemed to be ok as well. Miles took a deep breath as he crouched down and put his hands underneath to lift it. "Lift with your legs," he mumbled. To his complete and utter shock, he lifted the motorcycle effortlessly to an upright position. "*Huh*," he gasped. He could not believe how light the V4 was. "Amazing."

He quickly sat on the V4 and studied the controls more closely. He looked up to see that the red knight had not moved at all. He looked around, searching for a compartment, but he could not find anything. "Maybe he had it on him," he pondered out loud. Suddenly he heard the red knight's engine roar and the wheels skid on the pavement. "Uh-oh. He's gettin' antsy," Miles yelped. "This thing better start."

His motorcycle roared to life. A control panel lit up in

front of him just below the handle bars. He noticed it before but had no time to actually study the indicators on the screen until now. He saw the red knight lowering his glowing spear as the engine revved down the highway. He took one last glance at the screen but still found nothing that would indicate a weapon.

"Study time is over. *Move*." Miles yelled as he raced into gear back out on the highway.

The red knight raced straight towards Miles, his spear lowered. Miles had no choice but to quickly dodge to the right just in time as they flew past one another. The tip of the spear was just inches away from Miles as he sailed past. As he skidded around to a stop, the red knight did the same. Miles knew he would be coming back for another pass. He tried not to panic. He studied the screen in front of him as quickly as he could. There were symbols for all sorts of things but he could not decipher what they meant. "Oh, what the hell do all these things mean? Gigi?"

There was no answer though, and soon the red knight came racing towards him again. Miles decided not to charge him this time, and instead made the knight chase him. He quickly started hitting every symbol on the screen. Each one he pressed came to the forefront of the screen. Soon he realized he could see the read-out on the inside of his helmet shield. The first one read 'Core Data.' "No. Not that one," Miles said. The second one read 'Fuel and Range.' "Nope." Miles checked behind him. The red knight was gaining on him. The third symbol he pressed came up. It read 'Tactical.' "Now we're getting somewhere." He selected tactical on the screen and three choices came up. He was very confused by them all. The only indication on each selection was a direction. One simply read 'Forward', the other 'Horizontal' and the last 'Vertical.' Miles shook his head and as he rode as fast as he could down the straightaway. "What the hell kind of weapons are those?"

He thought for a moment. "What have I got to lose? I can't shake this guy. Forward it is." He selected the choice for forward and instantly a compartment opened below the screen console and a handle produced itself in his left hand. As soon as Miles gripped the handle, icy blue light shot from both ends. The front end of the handle produced the longest part of the glowing light and at the tip was a silver, razor-sharpened point. He had found his joust.

"Holy Toledo," he yelled. "Luke Skywalker, eat your heart out."

At that moment, the red knight pulled up and skidded to a halt. Miles instantly noticed that he had stopped pursuing him, so he skidded and turned a 180 in the road, screeching to a stop, too.

"I guess forward was the right one after all," Miles said out loud. He began to grow nervous again. He examined the glowing weapon in his leather grip. "I don't know anything about jousting. This thing looks really bad ass, but damn, this will tear a guy in half." He looked down the road towards the red knight, staring defiantly back at him, gripping his weapon. "What are we doing here?" Miles asked himself softly.

There was no answer though. Before he knew it, the red knight was careening down the open road towards him again. Miles instinctively hit the gas and roared towards him as well. Both spears were lowered and both riders raced at top speed towards one another in an epic flash of red, purple, and icy blue. Miles did all he could think to do to keep from getting gouged by a speeding blade. He swung his spear at the last second to knock the charging red knight's blade to the side. The two jousts flashed in brilliant light as they collided in the air. Both riders skidded around to a momentary stop and then spun around to face-off again.

The red knight charged with his spear directly in front of him. His engine roared in the night air. The tires squealed on the pavement. Miles tried to think of what might happen next. He knew the red knight would not let him bat his spear away a second time. He was right. In a flash, the red knight produced a second part of his weapon. Out from the sides of the spear came two more spears that reached twenty feet or more on either side. His weapon was now formed into the shape of a T. The glowing, icy blue bar of the weapon came flying directly at

Miles' head. He quickly lowered his spear and ducked his head just in time. He nearly lost control of his V4, but carefully spun around to prepare for the next wave.

"Now we know what horizontal means," Miles said bluntly. "He'll see that coming though." He thought fast. There had to be a way to gain the upper hand. There was one more weapon left but Miles had no way of knowing what it would do without trying it.

The red knight spun around, his weapon still fully extended in the T-shape. His red-leathery gloves gripped around the handle. Miles tried to think as quickly as he could. The engines roared, the tires began to spin again, and smoke billowed behind them. At that moment, Miles regained his confidence. He formed a plan in his mind. *This has to work*, he thought to himself. He revved up his engine and threw the bike into gear and went racing towards the red knight.

The red knight seemed surprised in seeing Miles leading the charge instead of himself. He threw his V4 into gear and went flying towards Miles. He tilted his weapon and the tip scraped along the pavement, sending up an incredible trail of sparks, in an attempt to intimidate and distract Miles.

Miles ignored it and called up the tactical screen on his helmet. Both riders lowered their spear as they sped towards one another. At the final moment, Miles selected the vertical weapon. As he was hoping, the V4 ejected Miles straight up into the air. The red knight's charging spear and extended blade went right underneath Miles and over his V4. At the same instant, Miles swung his joust as hard he could and smacked the red knight directly across his back, sending him sailing over the front of his bike. The red V4 went flailing end over end like a bouncing football. The red knight's joust caught in the dirt and sent him sailing into the air like a champion pole vaulter.

Miles fell perfectly back down on his speeding V4 and skidded to a stop. He glanced over his shoulder to see the knight sailing through the air and his V4 tumbling down the road. The knight fell to the ground in agony and his V4 exploded on final impact. Almost as quickly as Miles stopped, the glowing joust retracted back inside the handle and then put itself away inside the hidden compartment. Miles sat stunned, knowing he had just defeated the red knight.

He watched as the red rider stumbled and tried unsuccessfully to get to his feet hundreds of yards away. "I forgot to tell you," Miles yelled out. "I was all-conference on my college baseball team too!"

Just then he noticed the woman in the black mask again. She stood alone on the side of the road, her black cape flowing in the wind. Miles shut off his V4 and got off and walked towards her. She stood motionless and stared at him, her eyes showing no emotion.

"It's you again," Miles began. "Who are you?"

The woman said nothing. He halfway expected her to disappear again, but this time she did not. She just stood silently looking at him. He stood on the road only feet from her.

"You watched the whole thing, didn't you?" he asked. "You've been following me this whole time." He thought for a moment. He knew there must be a reason why he kept seeing this masked woman. "Are you the reason I'm here? Do you know how to get me back?" She stared at him without saying a word. Her eyes looked past him and out into the dark open field. Miles looked over his shoulder at the red knight who was still struggling to get up way out in the field. He chuckled a bit as he watched. "I've played many a game of chess lady, but this is ridic…" He looked over again at the masked woman, but she was gone.

Miles put his hands on his hips and just shook his head. "I'm not one for long conversations either, sweetheart. Hope you enjoyed the show!" he yelled even louder. He walked back over to his V4 and started it up.

"Damnit," he muttered to himself. Then he sped off into the night, down the highway back towards Bangkok.

Keith R. Rees

Chapter 5
The Rook

The smell of the ocean air wafted into Miles' nostrils as he rode along the darkened road towards Bangkok. He could tell he was close to the sea but he could not see it in the dark. If it were not for the hum of the motor he knew he could probably hear the waves crashing ashore as he rode past.

To his surprise, the engine suddenly shut off and he glided to a stop on the side of the road. "What the hell happened?" he asked out loud. He tapped on the screen in front of him and selected 'Fuel and Range.' The red indicator flashed 'Empty' over and over again. "Of course," he smirked. "2065, and you can still run out of gas."

He took a deep breath and removed his helmet. He looked around him but there were no lights or businesses anywhere; only the glow of the sky up ahead where the city began. It did not take long before he noticed the sound of the waves nearby.

"I knew it," he whispered to himself. "Might as well go see it even if it is the middle of the night."

He stumbled over a few rocks as he walked towards the sounds of the sea. Soon, he found the edge of a narrow strip of sandy beach and he could see the small white caps breaking ashore in the darkness. He took in another deep breath, his lungs soaking in the salty air. He was so weary. Suddenly, he felt like he could fall right there on the tiny beach and go to sleep. The sounds of the waves alone could knock him out in seconds. He began to think about his kids and his wife Vicky again. The more he did the sadder he became. He shook his head as he stared towards the infinity of the darkened sea.

"What am I doing here? When am I going to wake up from this madness?" He glanced over his shoulder towards the glowing lights of Bangkok. All he could do was shake his head again. He felt like he could cry but he was too weary to. "I have to get back to Vicky. I can't take this anymore."

From the corner of his eye he saw some headlights coming down the road and began to slow as they neared him. Soon, the glider stopped directly behind his V4 on the other side of the road. Miles looked at the car curiously. *Who could be stopping at this hour?* he wondered. He halfway expected it to be Gigi, but instead of a woman there was a young man inside the glider. "Man, the natives sure are friendly around here," Miles blurted out. He began to walk back over the rocks towards the glider.

The young man emerged and called out, "Mr. Miles? You out there?"

Miles recognized him instantly. Still dressed in his chauffer's outfit and black hat was Chen, the young man from the airport. "Chen? Is that you?" He removed his hat and waved for Miles to come over. "Wow man, that's some service you provide. They should give you a raise."

"Hello, Mr. Miles," he greeted cheerfully. "You need lift?" He glanced over at the motorcycle shining in the headlights. He could see how scratched up it was. "Oh. Fancy schmancy. You got nice wheels, Mr. Miles. But what happen? You look like you crash. You okay?"

"Yeah, I'm alright. It's outta gas though." Miles looked at him curiously. "How'd you find me way out here? At this late hour? By the way, what time is it anyway?"

"Just after four," Chen replied. "I drop off fare in Chonburi. Now I'm on way back."

"Workin' the graveyard, huh? I hear ya buddy." Miles grabbed his helmet off the motorcycle. "I guess I could use a lift if you don't mind."

"Oh, not at all Mr. Miles. Hop in."

They both got inside the glider and it took off by itself. Chen sat in the back seat along with Miles. Miles chuckled to himself. "They send a taxi driver to drop off a fare but you don't actually have to drive, huh?"

Chen laughed. "Oh. They send me along because old lady need help with bags. So, I get easy tip but long ride back. Lucky I find you."

"Yeah, lucky me," Miles said with a hint of sarcasm. He was a bit suspicious though. "I don't know, Chen old buddy. Sure is quite a coincidence to me. Don't smell right." He shrugged his shoulders though. After the night he had been having so far, he was not going to ask too many questions. "A ride is a ride I guess. Beats walkin'."

"Hey, you want some rock 'n roll?" Chen switched on some music from a panel in front of him. "I love twentieth century rock music. You like?"

Miles listened to the music and instantly knew what it was. He began to laugh out loud.

"This is rock band from Canada. They called Rush!" Chen was very excited. He pretended to play air guitar to the song.

Miles laughed even harder. "Yeah, I know who it is. Ha ha. Interesting choice though. *A Passage to Bangkok,* huh? Really? Very funny. Are we making any 'stops' along the way?" Miles kept laughing. "You know what this song is about, don'tcha?"

Chen sang along with his broken accent as he continued playing air guitar. "We hit the stops along the way. *Weeee* only stop for the *best*." He was really getting into the guitar rhythm. "Yeah, Mr. Miles. It's about rock and roll. And riding a train to Bangkok. You get it? We riding to Bangkok, too."

Miles could not help but laugh. "Yeah, I get it. You seem a little *too* wound up buddy. Maybe you've made a few stops along the way already, huh? Am I right?" Miles kidded and elbowed him a light jab.

Chen settled down. He obviously had no clue why Miles was kidding him though. He just liked the old song. He became serious. "What happened out there, Mr. Miles? You find trouble?"

"I guess you could say that," Miles chuckled. "Either that or Darth Vader's psychotic cousin." Chen looked at him blankly. "Doesn't matter. I'm glad you happened along, though. The airport is where all this craziness started, so that's probably the best place to head back to."

"Somebody after you?" Chen asked.

"Ha! Yeah. Everywhere I turn it seems."

Suddenly, the glass in the back window shattered. *"Shit!"* they both yelled.

Miles ducked behind the seat and glanced behind them. Inside another glider was the red knight firing a weapon at them. "Yep, right on cue."

"Who *that*?" Chen screamed.

"The psychotic *cousin*."

"*Who?*" Chen had no idea what he was saying.

"The knight from *hell*." Miles yelled back. "Can't this thing move any faster?"

"Yes. I go." Chen leapt into the front seat and ducked down as far as he could and put the glider into manual drive. He punched the accelerator and immediately the glider went speeding away from the red knight.

"Atta boy, Chen. Lose this sucker." Miles could hear the firing of the weapon and the strange hissing sound as the ammunition flew past. "*Geez*. What the hell kinda gun is that?"

They raced down the country road as a hail of gunfire rained down on them. All the windows shattered and Miles was covered in glass, still crouched on the floorboards.

"Why they shooting at us?" Chen screamed from a crouched position behind the wheel.

Miles rolled around on the floor as the glider careened down the road. "Oh, I think he's just a *wee* bit sore at me."

"What you do, Mr. Miles?"

Miles sheepishly grinned and yelled back over the seat, "Well, let's see. I sort of destroyed his Ferrari sports bike and I kinda sorta used him as my own personal baseball."

"That not good," Chen panicked.

"Umm, no." Miles peeked over the seat. The red knight was still right on top of them. "Can't you lose him?"

Chen was an expert driver. Soon they were back in the

city. He zipped down streets and back alley-ways, and before long, the red knight was no longer behind them.

"Nice drivin', Chen old buddy," Miles commended him. "I think we lost him."

"It safer here. Crazy people like that won't go firing guns in crowded city like this. The police are too good. Very strict." He sat up in his seat and slowed the pace of the glider. "I think we safe now. I get you back. She won't follow us anymore."

Miles climbed into the passenger seat up front. He looked at Chen cockeyed. *"She?"* Miles immediately knew something was amiss. Chen had a sheepish look on his face when he realized his slip of the tongue. "Come on man, what's going on here? You know who that was?" He could not help but think how convenient it was for Chen to just happen by in the middle of nowhere. He did not know what to think of Chen any longer. It just did not add up.

Miles thought about all the nifty moves the red knight had made on the V4 and how crafty she was in the riding moves. "*She,* huh?"

Chen tried to ignore him though. "We almost here," he said.

"Almost where? This isn't the airport, dude." Miles looked at him more sternly. "How did you know that was a she?"

Chen drove the glider down an area that was away from

the lights and glitz of the city. It appeared to be a more serene and calm neighborhood and was covered with trees and foliage. Miles became less and less trusting as the glider slowed down as it rolled through the winding narrow roads.

"Hey man, I thought we were going to the airport," Miles asserted.

Soon, the car stopped next to a cobbled walkway. At the end of the walkway, adorned with vines and green trees, was an old rounded turret about thirty feet high. It resembled a rook on the chess board. At the bottom of the rook was a single door. Miles slumped in his seat. He knew right away he was not going where he wanted. He had no choice but to go along with it.

"This isn't fair, man. Even in Thailand you got to know this shit ain't cool."

Chen got out of the glider, straightened his uniform, and put on his black hat. Once again, he settled into his role as servant and chauffeur. He opened the door for Miles. Reluctantly, Miles got out of the car and stood on the cobbled walkway.

"So, now what?" Miles asked in exhaustion.

Chen directed him towards the door of the turret. "This way."

Miles' eyes widened. "You want me to go in there? I don't think so. I don't wanta go in there."

But Chen quietly kept extending his hand towards the door. Miles hands began to shake. He was not liking this at all.

What would he find on the other side of the door?

"Use your thumb on the scanner," Chen instructed. "Please, this way."

Miles rolled his eyes and reluctantly walked towards the door. He had a very somber look on his face as he stared down at the thumb scanner on the wall next to the door. He looked back at Chen, but he was already gone.

"Oh, terrific," he drawled. "Sneaky bastard. Those damn things are too quiet." He forced a sarcastic smile and shook his head, "I guess I'm going in." He pressed his thumb to the plate and immediately a green light came on. Then he heard the metal door being unlatched automatically. "What a shock. They have my thumbprint." Miles pushed the large door open and stepped inside.

As soon as he stepped inside, his clothes changed back to the old street clothes that he had on before. Miles froze for a moment, still startled by how changes like that occurred. The door closed by itself behind him. He fully expected to see a stairwell leading to the top of the tower, but instead all he saw was a stone wall. Off to the side there were steps, but did not lead upward. It was a rounded stone stairwell that led downward, and it was the only passage he could take. He walked over to the top of the steps and tried to look around the curved walls to try to see where it went, but all he could see was a lighted torch on the side of the wall. He thought the entire walkway would be lit with torches, but it appeared to be pitch black beyond where he was standing.

"I guess I'm supposed to carry this one," Miles said staring at the burning torch. "What? Did I step back into the medieval period or something?" He grabbed the torch from the wall and held it tightly in his hands as he tried to peer down the stairwell. "Whatever. So, I'm carrying a torch down a darkened stairwell. Nothing strange about that."

He began to walk down, one step at a time. The walls were all the same; dark and damp, and all appeared to be very old. He rounded the staircase after what seemed to be two or three flights before he finally came to a landing. On the wall were two swords, criss-crossed in the shape of an X. They were gold and silver and the handles were very ornate in appearance.

"Fancy," Miles said to himself. He raised the torch to look around the room. It was no more than seven or eight feet square. There was nothing else on the walls other than the two swords, and in the corner was another set of stairs that looked to be heading straight down instead of spiraling. He was not too keen on going any further, though. He decided to go back up the curved stairs and see if he could find a way out the turret door where he had entered.

As he walked, the light shone on the wall where the swords were. One of the swords was suddenly missing. Miles froze in his tracks. "Oh crap," he whispered. In an instant, the sound of a blade slicing through the air wisped past his head and clanged against the stone wall. There was another thrust of the blade, then another. Miles instinctively held the torch out and tried his best to block every blow of the sword. Holding the sword in the glow of the light was the red knight, still wearing the riding helmet and dressed in fiery red.

"You again?" Miles gasped. He backed away slowly, holding the torch up as his defense. He was a few feet from the other sword. He had to figure out a way to get to it without being cut down.

The red knight swiped and swished the sword in the air like an expert dueler taking aim.

"I guess you're still sore at me," Miles quipped. He was terrified, but sarcasm was his way of coping at the moment. The knight swung the sword in an arc towards his head. He blocked it just in time with the wooden torch. Sparks of fire flew everywhere upon the impact. "I'll take that as a yes."

Miles flung the torch straight at the knight, and she backed away just enough for Miles to jump over to the wall and grab the other sword. The torch lay on the floor as the two slowly walked side to side with their swords up.

Miles thought about how he had left the helmet in the gravity glider with Chen and how his clothes had changed back to ordinary ones once he stepped inside. He had no protection at all. Yet the red knight still had the leathery outfit like he once had on. The same outfit that could take a burning slide on the pavement at a hundred miles per hour. Plus, she still had on her helmet.

"I think you have the advantage here, sweetheart," Miles said, trying to buy some time. The sword felt awkward in his hand. It was heavier than he had imagined. He had never held one before, much less used one in combat. "You know, you are a great rider. You had some awesome moves back there. Very impressive. What do you say we talk this over, huh? I'll buy you a latte. They still have Starbucks these days?"

The red knight said nothing. She kept her sword at the ready. She maneuvered from left to right, parried and thrusted. Miles barely blocked her thrusting sword and knocked it away. The blades clanged together as they danced in the firelit corridor. He was astonished at how well he was able to fend her off. He was defending each blow he took, yet he felt clumsy and awkward with the sword. With each slash of the blade, she came closer to striking a blow.

The sword began to feel heavy in his hands. Sweat poured from his face and his clothes became wet with sweat. His wrists became sore. He did not know how much longer he could keep fending off her attacks. The blade went slashing in front of his belly. He jumped back as it just missed his flesh, but ripped through the fabric of his shirt and sports coat that was hanging loosely from his exhausted frame. He seized on the moment and in desperation thrust his sword forward. He caught the red knight directly below her right shoulder. He fully expected the blow would wound her, but instead her red armor flicked the blade harmlessly away. It was the best opportunity he had. He clearly did not want to hurt anyone, much less impale them with a sword, but he was given no choice. Now that the chance had presented itself, he had failed miserably. The red knight clearly had the upper hand and now Miles felt demoralized. How could he keep this up? He had only one other alternative.

The blades clanged together again, then a second and a third and a fourth time. Miles stumbled and scrambled to get to his feet. His mind raced to figure out how he could get out of his certain defeat. He tried to think, but everything in his mind was a blur. All he could see was the fiery red menace swirling a sword around his head in the glimmer of the torchlight.

The torch! Miles was elated as he caught sight of the wooden handle burning on the stone floor. His eyes were diverted as the red knight swished her sword to make a head blow. Instinctively, Miles dropped to the floor. When he rose, he tackled her, pinning her arms and sword behind her and against the wall. "I've had enough of this," he shouted. In a flash, he pulled her in and then flung her body as hard as he could, sending her sliding backwards on the floor. He ducked and rolled away from her, and at the same time, grabbed the torch and leapt down the darkened stairs.

He moved like he had never moved before, racing down the stone staircase three and four steps at a time. He could hear the charging footsteps behind him, but clearly thought he had the advantage as he could see where he was going while she was chasing him in the darkness. He had no idea where the stairs were leading, or if he was simply heading down a dead end. If he were, he would turn and face his fate. If not, hopefully he could find a way to lose the red knight once and for all.

He rounded a corner, flying on foot as fast as he could. Before he knew it, he crashed into a large wooden door. "Holy crap." He pulled on the large wooden lever and it miraculously opened. He dashed inside and quickly closed it behind him. He could hear the sound of the knight crashing into the door on the other side. He quickly shoved his sword inside the door handle and jammed it against the wall. The sword clanged against the wall as the red knight desperately shoved on the door, but the sword held steady.

Confident with the door-jam, he quickly walked down the narrow corridor. Soon, the hallway opened and before long he could see light up ahead. He came into a large, empty chamber that was as musty and gray as the rest of the castle. It almost seemed like he was in the Dark Ages and was trapped inside a medieval fortress. The only thing that reminded him he was in the future was the CommVice on his wrist.

Then, he noticed a small screen on the wall of the chamber. Suddenly the screen flickered and Gigi appeared on it. Miles was startled. He was actually glad to see her.

"*Gigi*," he exclaimed. He kept expecting her to appear in full form before him, but her face remained on the wall-screen. "Boy, am I glad to see you." He slumped against the wall and tried to rest.

"Hello, Miles," was all Gigi would say.

Miles was perturbed at her casual greeting. *"Hello?"* He pushed away from the wall and stared directly at her on the screen. "*Where the hell have you been?* I'm freaking trapped in here, pal! And that red *bitch* is in here, too!" He began to pace back and forth in front of the screen, still looking back down the corridor to make sure the red knight had not broken through the door. "And she's really not one for conversation, I can tell you that. All she wants to do is run me over or slice me up." He became more impatient with Gigi's silence with each passing moment. "Well, come on! Tell me how to get out of here. She's right on my ass." He wiped the sweat from his forehead and continued to catch his breath. "I'm really a lousy fighter, Gigi. And by the way, I *suck* at fencing. It was no wonder my high school PE coach always told me, 'Stick to bowling.'"

"You say you are not a good fighter?" Gigi finally asked. "I think you can prove otherwise."

Miles stopped pacing and looked at the screen. He could

not believe what he was hearing. "Oh no. What are you up to? Every time you say something squirrely like that I get thrown back to the wolves. Enough challenges already. Haven't I met your damn standards by now?"

Gigi was unswerving. "You have done well in the arts of the modern world. But now it's time to learn the ways of the past."

Miles dropped the torch and tried to reason with her. "No, no, no. Listen, I've gone through all your little games and challenges. I've beaten all the pieces on the chess board. I've taken them all!"

"Have you?" Gigi asked. "Take off your CommVice. Place it in the slot below the screen."

Miles' blood ran cold in his veins. He knew she was not going to let him out that easily. His hands began to shake as his worst fears were confirmed. He was not done yet. "OK, you're right. If we are playing chess, there is still the king and queen left on the board. I get that. But can't we just call it a day? Maybe we can all just sit down, talk it over with a nice glass of wine. Whadd'ya say?"

Gigi only repeated herself. "Place the CommVice into the slot, Miles."

Reluctantly, he took off his device and walked over to the screen on the wall. Below it was a small square-shaped slot carved into the stone, the same size as the face of the Comm-

Vice. He took a deep breath and turned the device around and placed it into the slot.

The entire room instantly transformed from a dark and musty stone chamber into an enormous, colorful expanse. The room lit up, the floor changed to marble, and the walls sparkled with light. There were crystal chandeliers, ornate curtains, and a decadent set of rounded staircases cascaded downward from both sides of the grand hall. The entire room was bathed in soft tones of brown and beige and orange. Emeralds and rubies glistened on the walls and the furnishings. It appeared to be the most ornate and decorative of palaces, and he was standing in the middle of all its grandeur. His eyes were amazed as they took in the splendor of the large room. On either side of the room were two consoles that seemed to be out of place. He wondered what they were.

H looked down at himself and realized his clothes had changed along with the virtual room. He was now shirtless and only wearing a pair of dark fighter's shorts. A colorful plaid sash was wrapped around his waist, and a matching sash wrapped around his head, draped down one shoulder, and hung in front.

Gigi's hologram was now standing beside him. She noticed how curiously he looked at his attire. "It is called a *pakama*. It is the traditional dress that participants adorn themselves with before they take part in the Muay-Thai."

"Muay-Thai? What is that, some kind of dance?"

"No, it is the ancient Thai form of martial arts in the kingdom. It is known as the 'art of the eight limbs.' It is a combination of the fists, elbows, knees and shins."

Miles was incredulous. "*Martial arts?* I don't know anything about martial arts. And I definitely don't know any of this Muay-Thai thing. I'd rather hang onto my eight limbs if you don't mind. How 'bout if we just go back to the beach and ride V4's again? That would be cool with me."

"Go over to the console on the wall," she instructed. "Place your hands together in the center."

Miles shook his head. He knew he had to do as she instructed. It was the only way he knew that he could possibly be allowed to return home. He had to complete the full challenge. He slowly walked over to the lightly colored stone console on the wall. In the center was a round inverted disc with a symbol carved into it. It depicted a pair of hands outstretched, side by side. He looked over his shoulder at Gigi and she nodded for him to proceed.

As he placed his hands side by side together inside the disc, he felt his body being pulled in as if by a powerful force. His hands stuck to the wall; he could not move. His eyes closed as he felt a wave of sensation cascade over his entire body. It was a power he had never felt before. It only lasted a few seconds and suddenly his hands were freed and his eyes flashed open. He whirled around to face Gigi with a defiant look in his eyes.

"I know, Muay-Thai," Miles announced confidently. "As if I've known all my life."

Gigi motioned to her right. Standing on each staircase were the two bishops from the sphere chasers. They were both dressed in the traditional *pakama* as well, one in brightly adorned golden yellow and the other in silvery blue. "Show them," she commanded.

"What?" Miles shouted aghast. He was shocked to see them again.

"Did you think you were done with them?" Gigi mocked. "Did you think it would be that easy to get to the king and queen? You are still in the rook!"

Miles walked to the center of the room and faced the bishops. Each one removed the *pakama* from their head and flung them over the railings. Their muscled, chiseled chests glistened with sweat. They stepped off the final stair and assumed a fighting stance. Miles knew he was in for a fight. He removed his *pakama* and tossed it to Gigi. "Hang on to that for me."

He assumed a fighting stance and faced his opponents. "Two against one, huh? Whatever." Miles' confidence was sky high, and rightly so. As the three fighters engaged, it was obvious right away that Miles was up to the challenge. He balanced on his feet and moved like an expert. Fists and feet flew with fury, but Miles deflected every blow each man attempted. With clinching fists, he swiveled and balanced and danced with each advancing blow. "Come on," he taunted them, "is that all you got?"

With that Miles took a shin to the head from the fighter in silvery blue. He stumbled back on his heels and tried to shake the dizziness from his head. He was shocked by the severity of the kick. He quickly got back into stance, even angrier. He returned the favor by giving a shin to the chest of the same fighter and then a quick elbow to the face. The man staggered back with a bloody nose but continued to fight.

The men moved about the room trading kicks and fists and knee blows and sharp elbow punches. They tried to go for Miles' knees to make him fall but he was too quick. He moved like a stealthy cat, dancing away from their every move. He bobbed and weaved like a prize fighter in the ring, and with each flailing punch, Miles landed a jab to the jaw, a knee to the gut, and then a crushing shin to the head. The fighter in golden yellow suddenly disintegrated into ash as soon as the foot struck his head.

Miles was briefly stunned at seeing the man disappear, but soon had fists and feet flying at him from the other fighter. He turned his attention to him and began to fight one on one.

He found it easier to focus on one opponent but this made

it even tougher as the man fought him with renewed vengeance. They traded kicks and barbs all around the room again. Miles became weary from all the blows to the head he was taking, but each time he gave as good as he got. He hoped with each strike that his opponent would turn to ashes too, but no such luck. The fight intensified with each moment.

The fighters began to duel with their fists on the staircase. Every hop up the stairs was accompanied by a jab with a fist. Miles tried to throw in a kick, but instead kicked the railing. He stumbled and winced in pain. He did his best to balance on one foot as his opponent continued to rain down blows on him. He had the upper ground on Miles, and clearly was getting the best of him. Miles tried desperately to counter, but the pain in his foot was becoming too much. In a last desperate act, he planted himself on both hands with his feet in the air. The man stopped briefly and looked at him curiously from a higher step. Miles seized on the open opportunity and swirled his body on his fingertips and landed a crushing blow to the head with his good leg. The stunned fighter went flailing over the side, crashing to the floor. As soon as the man hit the marbled floor he disappeared into ashes.

Miles stared at the floor in astonishment. He pushed off with his hands and landed on the stairs on one leg. He limped back down the stairs to the bottom, still staring at where the man disappeared. He limped over to where Gigi was watching.

His leg was still in pain but felt better as he walked it off. Gigi looked at him, unimpressed.

"The railing got me," he said grimacing. He motioned to the floor where the piles of ashes lay. "Whoops."

Motioning to the other console on the far wall, Gigi said, "Go to the console and place your hands in it."

"Now wait a minute," he protested, "How 'bout a breather for just one second? *Geez*."

"Why do you want to rest when you are so near to the end?" Gigi asked.

"I am?" he asked hopefully. "You mean I'm almost out of this mess? What could possibly be left though?"

As soon as he asked the question, eight figures appeared on the stairs, four on each side. All of them were brandishing swords and staves. They raised them in sync, and they looked perfectly arranged with a feathered spectacle of weapons. Miles stepped back. He looked at the incredible ensemble with disbelief. "Eight of them?" he shrieked. "Don't tell me it's the pawns again!"

"The pawns," Gigi echoed his statement. "They come ready, armed for the Krabi-krabong."

"Oh no, what's that?" Miles asked bewildered.

"Place your hands in the console," she repeated.

"What? Don't you think this might be a little one-sided?"

Gigi ignored him though. "I would suggest you do it

now."

Wearily, Miles hobbled over to the other console. The last thing he wanted to do was fight again, much less against eight much younger, angrier people wielding long knives and clubs. He was ready to give up, too tired to go on. He stared hopelessly at the beige console on the wall. Inside the inverted disc was the symbol of a slightly curved long knife and a staff. He took another deep breath and placed his hands inside the circle and closed his eyes.

A wave of sensational energy shot through his body. Even though his eyes were closed, he could see clouds and light moving over a vast landscape in accelerated motion. It was so fast it was if time were moving. Years became seconds. He saw the faces of his three kids even though he knew that was not right. At this point he only knew two of them. Yet, he saw all three of them. Then he saw the face of his wife as the clouds and sunrises and sunsets continued to soar past at light speed.

His body shook. His eyelids flickered. Then suddenly his hands were forced away from the console. A feeling of renewed adrenaline came over him. He felt stronger. His foot was no longer sore. His attire had changed again. He was adorned in the traditional outfit of the *Krabi-krabong*. The matching top and bottom were of royal blue and a majestic stripe of purple encircled his sleeves. He wore a thin headband of the same vibrant purple with thin strings that tied and hung down the back of his neck.

In one hand was the traditional elongated and slightly curved sword called the krabi. In the other he held the krabong, a staff that measured a little more than four feet. It was wrapped with thin strands of multiple colors in three separate places along the shaft of red, white, blue, white, and red.

He turned to face his opponents with a fierce look. They were all dressed in the same attire as was Miles. The stripes on their sleeves were the same as when he faced them at the Great Swing. There was one pawn each wearing a headband and stripes of simmering red, electric flame, tangerine orange, emerald green, metallic blue, neon yellow, sharp turquoise and glowing maroon. Miles walked over casually and stood defiantly at the foot of the two staircases in the center. His young adversaries looked at him with awe but with determination.

Miles held his weapons at his sides and looked at each row of pawns on the steps. He gave them a look as confidently and curiously as ever, as if he were ready to go outside and play tag with them. "Well, boys and girls, what are you waiting for?"

They screamed and rushed down the staircases in unison. Miles took his stance and raised his weapons. With machine-like efficiency, he thwarted each blow from them as they attacked from all sides. Swords, staves and bodies flew in every direction. It was mayhem, and in the center of it all was Miles, effortlessly fighting off every blow from a staff and every thrust from a sword with his own.

He found out right away that they were not just kids. They were expertly trained in martial arts and they were unafraid. They were just as coordinated and fluid as they were at the Great Swing. Miles was struck by the contrast of these new challenges to the ones he faced prior. Gone were the gravity gliders, the sphere chasers, and the concept racing motorcycles. Here it was the old way. Hand to hand and sword to sword. The agile and the swift are the victor. The cunning and the clever prevail.

They fought all around the great hall, up and down the staircases as they bounced off the walls and hurled themselves in any defensive manner. The sound of wood cracking on wood and the clang of swords engulfed the virtual fighting arena.

Sweat poured down Miles' face, yet he was not tired. He was invigorated. He had never been in a fight of this magnitude, ever. Yet he was unscathed by their attacks.

One of the stronger boys went to make a crushing blow to Miles' head with his krabong, but Miles blocked it just in time. His teeth gritted and he screamed in Miles' face. Miles held his ground and fought him off but he knew he had to free himself soon or he would be struck by one of the other seven. Miles finally overpowered him and threw him back into three of the other fighters. Suddenly Miles felt a staff crack across the back.

He flung his sword to block another, then his staff to block again. A rip slashed through his clothes. A sharp pain tore through his flesh. He had been sliced along the side of his torso. He felt the searing pain left behind by the blade. A red stain of blood formed on his fighting attire.

He staggered to his feet, expecting to feel more blows from both sword and staff, yet a second wind of fury came over him and he fought with even more determination. He quickly gained the upper hand and landed blows directly on one opponent after another. With each decisive strike, the pawns disintegrated into ashes one by one, just as the bishops before. Soon, he was down to five, then to four. Then, after a flurry of metal and splintered wood, Miles faced the remaining two.

The blood stain on his clothing became larger and he could feel the blood dripping down his chest. He licked the sweat from his lips and flipped the tassels of his headband behind his neck. With two quick strikes, the fighter in tangerine orange was gone. All that remained was the littlest of the pawns, who wore emerald green. He could tell she was a young girl and that she was quivering as she stood with her sword and staff raised. Miles came out of his fighting stance and looked at her.

"That is enough," Miles finally said. He dropped his krabi and krabong.

Suddenly, the entire great hall transformed from the ornate grandeur back into the drab and dank stone corridor. The image of the young girl fighter instantly disappeared. Miles looked over to where Gigi was standing. To his surprise, he also saw the masked woman in black. She stood near the screen and slot on the wall, and in her hands, was the CommVice.

Then, she spoke the only words he ever heard her say. "That is enough." As soon as she spoke, Gigi and the masked woman in black both disappeared.

Chapter 6
The King

Miles stood alone in the empty stone chamber. Only the light of the torch remained. He panted as he tried to catch his breath. His shoulders and his back ached, and the cut along his upper chest still stung. He did not think it was a deep cut, but was still a fairly large wound.

There was no sound at all. He thought about what had just happened. Who was the woman in black? Would he ever see her again? And what about Gigi? He kept expecting her to show up on the wall-screen or on his CommVice, but she did not. He picked the CommVice from the floor where the woman in black had vanished. He looked at the blank screen for a moment and sighed. "Forget it," he mumbled and tossed it aside back on the floor.

He stood up straight and then he heard a large door being opened. At the other end of the corridor, a light came cascading into the darkened corridor. A shadowy figure appeared in the doorway and Miles had to hold his hand up to the glare. The figure walked forward until he could finally see who it was. The oldest of the pawns emerged from the light, still dressed in sleek black with tangerine orange stripe. A long sword extended from her hand.

Miles sighed heavily. His shoulders slumped in weariness. She was the last person he wanted to see. "You again, huh? No more, alright? I see you didn't disintegrate." Miles was beyond exasperated. "I'm not fighting anymore, you understand me? You win!"

The tall girl swished her sword in the air, and then to his surprise she sheathed it on her side. It was the first time he had gotten a long look at one his foes. She was a young Thai woman, no more than twenty years old. Her hair was sleek and black and shoulder length, and in quite simple terms, strikingly beautiful. Miles' eyes widened. She was quite astonishing. She stood to the side and motioned for him to walk through the passage.

Miles slowly walked down the hallway and stopped momentarily to get a good look at the eyes of the young woman before him. Her face seemed so familiar to him. In that moment, he understood that she no longer meant him any harm. She motioned again with her hand for him to continue walking.

The light from the doorway became brighter as he came

closer. He had to shield his eyes as he walked through. Finally, he could uncover his eyes. He stood in a small chamber, ornately decorated just as the virtual great hall was before. In the room was finely made wooden furniture, mirrors for walls, crystal chandeliers and light fixtures. To one side was a finally polished credenza, carved with intricate designs on the front. On the top were crystal decanters filled with red wine and dark alcohol. Flowers were on countertops and fine leather sofas and chairs were placed in various spots around the room. The mirrors made the room look much larger than it was.

In the center of the room were two wooden armchairs with leather cushions that faced each other. They stood only a few feet apart. It looked as if there should be a table in between them, but there was not.

Miles looked all around the impressive chamber and nodded with weary satisfaction. He looked over his shoulder at the woman and said casually, "Nice place you got." But he soon found out it did not belong to her.

He turned around to see an old man on the other side of the room. Miles was startled and looked at him curiously. The man appeared to be in his sixties or seventies. He was nearly bald and wore a simple pair of thick, black glasses. He was wrapped in traditional formal Thai garments. They were light brown and draped at his feet.

"You are indeed an impressive adversary," the man said

to Miles' surprise. He halfway expected the elderly man to give an order to attack. Instead the man stood with a look of respect on his face. Miles was both relieved and confused. *Who is this man?* he wondered.

"Thank you," was all that Miles could think to say.

The old man tilted his head slightly and for a moment it looked as if he were going to smile. "I will echo the sentiments of my warriors, as one of them so graciously told you in the midst of battle. It is my honor."

Miles' eyes widened. He still did not know what to say. He felt he had heard those words spoken before but after all the chaos throughout the night he could not remember where.

"Um, well I..." he stuttered.

"See to his comfort," the man instructed.

Miles turned to see whom he was speaking to. Instead of the oldest pawn, he saw three young Thai girls dressed in servant's attire of white and gray. They bowed to the man and immediately directed Miles to another door off to the side.

Miles realized right away that he no longer had to fend for his life. He must have made it to his final destination in his trial, but as to where that was he still had no idea. He followed the servant girls into another ornately decorated room. He quickly surmised it was a fancy shower and dressing room.

He was able to take a nice long hot shower and then the servant girls dressed his wounds. He then put on traditional

Thai attire similar to that of the old man.

"You like?" one of the girls asked him hopefully. "You feel comfortable?"

"Yes, thank you," he replied.

They led him back into the fancy room where he first saw the man. He noticed him sitting in the center of the room in one of the two wooden chairs with leather cushion.

"I hope they have seen to your needs," the man spoke once again.

"Yes, it's very nice. Thank you." Miles was eager to get to the heart of the question and find out why he was here. He wanted to know why he had to go through such trials just to get to this place. However, he was distracted by a rather familiar aroma in the air, something that whetted his appetite almost immediately. "If you don't mind me saying, something smells *damn* good in here."

The man smiled, saying, "I knew that you must be famished. I'm having them prepare a meal for you."

"Mighty nice of you, Mister...um?" But the man did not answer. "I guess I could use a bite. Kinda smells like gumbo," Miles chuckled. He had no idea what they were preparing in the unseen kitchen, but his nose knew what it was smelling. It smelled fantastic. He scanned his eyes around the room once more. The crystal decanters caught his attention.

"We will share a drink," the man offered. "Gin and

tonic?"

Miles nodded approvingly. "Can't say no to that."

The man snapped his fingers and immediately one of the girls began to prepare two gin and tonics at the credenza. She brought them over and politely handed one to both the men. Miles took a long sip and sighed approvingly.

"I'm glad you approve," the man smiled. "Care for a game while we wait for our food?"

Miles gave him a puzzled look. He was in no mood for any more challenges or battles. Plus, he could not imagine what game he would play against the old man. There was nothing in the room that resembled a game. Perhaps it was a mind game, he thought. His mind was very confused and tired as it was already. Suddenly, the floor between the two wooden chairs opened and a transparent table appeared between them. The table glowed silver and white, and atop was an incredible crystal chessboard. The board was thick and appeared to be marble, except it was transparent and sparkled like fine glass. Each side of the board was lined with equally impressive chess pieces, all crystal and glassy in appearance. One set of pieces stood in shimmering silver, and the other in dazzling transparent white. It was the most incredible chessboard he had ever seen.

"Wow!" was all that Miles could muster.

The man motioned to the chair opposite him. "Please, join me."

Miles slowly sat down in the chair opposite the man, still looking at the chess pieces with amazement. He realized that the whole set, including the table, was virtual. He could pass his hand through the table and even the chess pieces. "This is amazing! But how can you play if you can't even pick up the pieces?"

"It's programmed to your mind," the man said without hesitation. "Once you decide on which piece you wish to play, you will be able to grasp and feel the desired piece and make your play. Try and focus on one piece."

Miles studied the chess pieces before him. The eight pawns were perfectly aligned on the front row, as were the pieces in the back row. He focused his mind on one piece and then attempted to grasp it. To his surprise, he was able to pick up one of the rooks on the corner. He held the tip of the rook between his fingers and then curiously waved his other hand through the transparent piece as if it were a ghost. "That's incredible." Miles was a little taken aback and quickly put the piece back on the chess board. When he did so, the square underneath the rook flashed briefly with light. "That's um, that's some chess board you got there."

"I am delighted that you approve," the man answered. "I will start the play."

"Of course," Miles accepted. He watched as the man moved his first pawn. The square underneath it flashed with light as it did before with Miles when the piece was placed down.

As they began to play, Miles still had plenty of questions. It was obvious that the man was not going to tell him who he was, at least not right away. So, he tried his best to fill in the other blanks.

"When I walked in here, it literally looked like a rook. What is this place?" Miles asked curiously.

"It is my home," the man responded plainly.

"You live in a castle? You must be someone of great importance around here."

"A man's home is his castle is it not? However, it's just the doorway that looks like a rook. The rest of the house is normal to me. It was built over an ancient fortress. You've seen some of the original corridors and rooms. So, that's why I had the rook built for my entry way. I like to build with a sense of humor and style."

Miles placed another piece on the chess board. "So, what was this all about tonight? Why were those people trying to kill me? What am I doing here?"

"All your questions will be answered, I assure you," the man began. "But first I wanted to see the man. The man of adventure. I wanted to see the mettle inside him." He placed another piece on his side of the board and took one of Miles' pawns. As soon as he did, the pawn disappeared. Miles was on the edge of his seat, barely paying attention to the game being played in front of him. "They were not trying to kill you."

Miles sat back in his chair somewhat startled. "Well it sure as hell seemed that way to me. And what do you mean, 'man of adventure'?"

"They were told that you were the adventurous type. That you liked to be daring and to try new and amazing things. They wanted to see for themselves. You obviously exceeded their expectations, or you would not be here now, I assure you."

"You mean like some nutcase that you can just egg on and chase around? *Who* told them that?" Miles asked breathtakingly. "I mean geez, I'm not some idiot looking for the next insanely wild way to die. Sure, I like an adventure as much as the next guy, but this was not exactly normal. Wouldn't you agree?" Miles leaned forward in his chair and looked at him seriously. "I'm in big trouble here. I don't how I got here but I'm stuck in this…this future! I don't belong here. Now I want some answers and I need to find out how to get back to 2005, back to my wife and kids. Something tells me you know those answers."

The man stopped playing the game for the moment. He studied Miles' face for what seemed like an eternity. Miles did not know what he was thinking, but one thing he did know was he was not getting up from his chair until he got some answers.

"You are right," he finally said. "I do apologize." Miles

set back in his chair with a look of hope on his face. Maybe he was finally getting somewhere. "I am an old man, and I had my wishes, but I must remember the position you are in. You are right, Miles. You don't belong here. And quite honestly, neither do I." Miles became even more confused.

"I don't understand," he said.

"The eight pawns that you encountered. They are my grandchildren. The two bishops are my nephews. I am quite proud of them all. I trained them myself. The girls who are helping you here are my nieces. They are all my family. But as you probably noticed, they do not look much like me at all. They all favor their grandmother."

"You're American, aren't you?" Miles interrupted.

"That is correct. I married a nice Thai woman many years ago after I migrated here."

Miles remembered the conversation he had with the old black man in the alley. "You mean the Great Migration?"

"Yes."

Miles was still curious about that. "What's the deal with that? Why did so many Americans leave our country? Was it really that bad in America?"

"Politics had taken its toll back then, I'm afraid," the man explained. "Bad politics. The freedom that our ancestors once left their homeland for was no longer there. It was there for the modern newcomers, but not for those of us who were born there and had lived there for generations. Our days were numbered back then. We were shut out and chastised if anyone dared to complain about being pushed aside. It was as if those who had been there for generations, whose parents and grandparents had fought and died for their country, no longer mattered. Political correctness took over and there was widespread fear among those who spoke out against special interests."

"I just can't believe that," Miles said sadly. "I know we had just been attacked, but in 2005, American pride was strong once again."

"Not even pride can withstand the flood from an arrogant policy of open borders. The poetic words displayed at the Statue of Liberty were taken too literally I'm afraid. Before they knew it, it was out of control. Those of us that could found refuge here in Bangkok and other places. It was not easy. The immigration guidelines were very strict, and still are. But with time, we were able to gain entry here."

"That's the most sobering thing I've ever heard." Miles took a long sip from his gin and tonic. "Can't be too bad here, though. You seem pretty well off to me. What exactly do you do here?"

The man took a sip of his drink and looked at Miles wryly. "Before the Great Migration in the twenties, I studied to be an engineer similar to my father. Except I studied civil engineering. That was one of the reasons we were allowed legal status in this country. I helped them rebuild their aging infrastructure and transformed Bangkok into the incredible city you have witnessed tonight."

"Incredible? It's astounding!" Miles exclaimed. "And you helped rebuild it?"

The man continued, "As a reward for my work, they sold me this property for a reasonable sum. I knew it was sacred to the people of Thailand, but that is the stature I had earned for myself here." He cleared his throat and pondered his chess pieces in front of him. "It was a blessing in disguise, having to come here. It enabled me to accomplish a great many things in my career and create a very satisfying family life. I will always be grateful for that." He briefly picked up the king chess piece and studied it for a moment, then placed it back down one space over. The square underneath the king flashed with light. "And now, I have accomplished something I never thought possible."

Miles looked at him firmly. "You mean time travel?" he asked curiously. The man looked at him as if he already knew what Miles was going to ask. Miles lowered his voice to a whisper. "What is the secret? Please sir, I must know how to get back."

The man answered without hesitation. "That I have already mastered. It was a certainty. What wasn't certain was this moment now. In order to get to this point, one would have to go through such incredible efforts, the most cunning of challenges, and have the most gifted set of abilities. Only then would I know that I had the right man. I did not know for certain until now." Miles looked at him blankly. *What could he possibly be saying?* "As I said before, you are indeed an impressive adversary."

This was getting too much for Miles. He wanted to get up from his chair and pace the floor, but instead he remained seated. "*Who are you?*" he asked shakenly.

"I have always wanted my father to show me the game of chess," the man finally said. Then he slowly spoke the next words Miles would never forget, "It is…my *honor*."

Miles sat stunned in his chair. He was speechless for what seemed like moments on end. The words *'my father'* kept rolling in his mind over and over. He felt dizzy and faint for a moment. His eyes fell upon the shimmering virtual chessboard. He slowly picked up the king in front of him. His mouth open and his mind awestruck, his eyes looked past the crystal king over towards the old man.

"*Cas?*" he finally gasped. His hands shook as he placed the chess piece back down on the board.

The man smiled at him. "Hello, Father."

The gravity of that statement shook Miles to the core. Not even twelve hours earlier, his son Casden was a toddler and could barely put three words together. He was still in diapers.

Now he was a grown man and well into his sixties. Miles sat there looking at Cas, speechless.

"Casden?" he said again. "It's really you?"

Cas nodded again. He knew he had to let the moment sink in for his father. Miles finally got up from his chair and walked over to his son. He knelt next to him.

"You are just a boy," Miles whispered. "I mean, you *were*." Then he remembered the phrase he used dozens of times a day. "My little man."

Cas chuckled approvingly. He knew then it really was his father. "Yes. That is what you called me."

Miles threw his arms around his son and hugged him tight. Cas turned and hugged him back saying, "It really is good to see you, Dad."

"It's good to see you, Cas. I don't know how you did it, but this is incredible."

All the pieces started to fall into place. Miles thought back to all the clues Cas had left behind as he went from one challenge to the next. Miles stood up and began pacing around the room.

"The boy at the airport. He knew who I was without even asking."

"Chen," Cas responded. "He is my grandson. Your great-grandson." Miles was flummoxed at the very statement. "The flight attendant on the plane is his sister. The old man selling amulets. And the woman who sold you the duck kabob, they are my in-laws."

Miles remembered one of the bishops had spoken to him as well. "The bishops, I mean your nephews. One of them smiled at me and said something in Thai only moments after we both came crashing to the ground. What did he say?"

"*Mạn pĕn keīyrti khrạb*," Cas responded. "It means it is his honor to see you."

"Chen said the same thing," Miles remembered. He shook his head in amazement. "I don't know what to say." He paced around some more, thinking of all that happened leading up to the present. "No wonder my fingerprint worked on the scanner. Programming the chessboard with my mind so I can play. And you knew exactly what my favorite drink was." He sniffed the fine aroma in the air once more. "And the dinner they are preparing. You're makin' gumbo, aren't you?"

"Chicken and sausage," Cas confirmed. "Your favorite."

"And I know I'm smellin' some cornbread," Miles laughed. "I had a feeling you had some New Orleans in you. I couldn't quite put my finger on it, but now it all makes sense."

As he spoke, the young girls walked out from the kitchen with three steaming hot bowls of chicken and sausage gumbo. Cas pushed the chessboard aside and it floated harmlessly away, suspended in midair. Seconds later a real wooden table covered in a fine white tablecloth appeared from the floor between the two chairs. It was carefully set with white cloth napkins, a single plate at each space, and three ice cold glasses of water. They placed a third chair at the table and Miles looked at it curiously. The girls delicately placed each bowl of gumbo on the plates and then placed a warm basket of corn bread on the side.

Just then, an older woman entered the room, looking a bit flustered, yet composed. She was dressed in a traditional Thai gown, but did not appear to be Thai herself. Miles did not recognize the woman at all, yet still she seemed oddly familiar. He assumed it was Cas' wife.

"Let me introduce you," Cas offered. "This is Milena, my sister-in-law."

"It's a pleasure to meet you, ma'am," Miles said politely.

Milena smiled sheepishly at him and answered, "It is mine as well. Please, dine with us."

"Of course. Thank you very much."

Miles sat down with them and began to slowly spoon the delicious gumbo into his mouth. "Mmmm," he sighed. "Just like home."

He and Cas both picked up a piece of cornbread at the same time and said in unison, "And some cornbread for dippin'." Miles and his son both laughed as they dipped the cornbread into the gumbo and took a huge bite. He smiled as if he were in Heaven. Wiping his mouth with his napkin, he asked, "Did you prepare this delicious meal, Milena?"

"Yes. I'm glad you like it." She slowly ate her gumbo and tried to hide the huge grin on her face.

"This is great, Cas. Nice to see that you brought some of old Louisiana with you." He ate some more of his gumbo as he spoke. "What about Gigi?"

Cas sat up in his chair and picked up his napkin. "What did you think of her?"

"Ha! More like a mother than a hologram. She was tough on me, I'll say. But I liked her. Good company."

Cas laughed and said, "I'm glad you did. I designed her myself."

Miles stopped eating for a moment and looked firmly at Cas. "You've done well here, Son. I'm proud of you. But don't you think I'm getting to cheat just a little? Seeing all this incredible stuff in the future, you all grown up and successful, long before I should?" He wiped his mouth with his napkin. "I don't want to sound ungrateful. I mean, what you've shown me is a true gift, but I'll be honest with you, Son. I'd rather see you grow up one day at a time. Witness how the boy becomes the man. Don't you agree?" Milena listened intently to what he was saying. She could tell the mood was about to change.

Cas put his spoon down and wiped his mouth as well. He took a slow drink from his glass of water. "Someone once told me, if you look at the sky day or night, you will always see a ray of hope, whether it's sunny or stormy, or the stars are shining bright." Miles looked at him puzzled. "Things happen for a reason, Father."

Miles thought for a moment, trying to see what Cas was getting at. He began to panic. He got up from the table and began pacing again. Milena became startled and put down her spoon. "There's something you are not telling me." He looked around the room looking for a way out. Miles looked at Cas with suspicion. "Where is your sister? Where's Vivian?"

"She's here in Bangkok, of course," Cas responded. "How else would I have nieces and nephews?"

"Right, right." Miles kept pacing, still unsatisfied. The comment distracted him somewhat. "So, we all just up and left America, the whole lot of us? I don't get that. Open borders or not, our country is the greatest in the world. What the hell would you *leave* for?" He shook his head in disgust. That was the least of his worries however. He needed to focus. "Sorry, sorry. I don't know what's been going on the last sixty years. You're right. You're right. Calm yourself, Miles," he scolded himself before his son could. "But still, there's something still not right here." The floating chessboard came into view. Miles eyed it and stared at one particular piece. He picked up the queen chess piece and held it in his shaking hands. "The queen. You said you married a Thai woman, Cas. Can I meet her?"

Cas nodded. "Of course, you can. But it's not my queen

you are wondering about, is it?" Miles stared at him with a nervous expression. He glanced down at the crystal chess piece in his hands. "It's yours."

Miles stood frozen in place. His heart began to pound in his chest as the chess piece fell from his fingers. Instead of disappearing the chess piece fell to the carpet with a thud. It had turned into a real piece of carved, crystal-like marble.

Miles turned to his son, his mouth agape and asked, "She's here?"

Chapter 7
The Queen

Miles felt a cold sweat forming on the back of his neck. His mind raced as it tried to catch up with his current reality. Was his wife Victoria really here in this time? The thought had not occurred to him until this moment.

"Is she really here?" he asked again. Cas stood silently. "If this is 2065, she would be...well into her nineties." The gravity of that thought was enormous. *Was he really going to see his wife sixty years older?* His mind ached.

He heard a door open, and as he turned around the room began to fill with one person after another. He watched as his future descendants came strolling into the large room. First, he saw Chen, still dressed in his chauffeur's uniform.

He tipped his hat towards Miles saying, "Hello again, Mr. Miles."

"Hey buddy," Miles smirked.

Then the two young men whom Gigi called the Bishops walked in. Cas's in-laws came in, as well as the flight attendant and finally the eight young teens that he first encountered at the market.

Miles nodded in approval at seeing them all. "You kids gave me quite a run out there. I'm very impressed with all of you. You are trained exceptionally well. I know your parents and your grandpa are proud." They smiled at him in appreciation. "I'm glad you went easy on me though, geez!" They laughed and giggled. "The whole ashes thing kinda freaked me out, though." They laughed even harder. "I really didn't want to kill anybody. I was glad I didn't. How was that possible anyway?"

Cas answered, "Virtual reality has made many advances over the decades."

"You can say that again."

"They were able to fight a simulated battle in another area that replicated the room you were in. They fought with your projected image. However, the blows they struck were real as you found out. When you landed decisive blows, they simply vanished and were eliminated."

"That's incredible," Miles said. "And the electric spheres and orbs and the ninja stars?"

"All real," his son replied. "Which is how I knew you were indeed my father and their grandfather. Only you would have been cunning enough and crafty enough to make it all the way through."

He walked over to the two young men who had fought him in the sphere chasers. "You two were exceptional up in the air. Got kind of hairy at the end though, didn't it?"

"Yes, sir," they both answered smiling.

"I hope you are both alright. That was a rough crash we had."

The two young men nodded and smiled at him. They were so nervous they did not know what to say.

Then one of the young girls who fought him along with the pawns approached him. "You're cut," she said pointing towards his chest. "Is it alright?"

Miles grinned and answered, "Yes, I think I'll make it, thank you."

"I was the one who did that. I am sorry."

He chuckled a bit. "Well, I'm the one who kicked you in the head. So, I'm sorry about that."

All the children laughed. "It's okay, we not feel anything using VR tactics."

"Lucky for you, huh?" Miles snickered. "Besides, no reason to be sorry. That was a pretty nice move you made."

Cas' father-in-law motioned to Miles and asked in his limited English, "You still have?"

Miles knew what he was referring to and pulled the

amulet from under his collar and showed the man. "Yes, I have it right here. Thank you again."

"Good, good," the man smiled approvingly.

Another older woman that Miles did not recognize came in, too. She stood next to Cas. "This is my wife, Kamlai. She also helped prepare the meal for us."

Miles clasped her hands and smiled at her, although he was confused as to why she did not dine with them as well. "It's a pleasure to meet you. Thank you for cooking. It was delicious."

"Always my pleasure, Mr. Devereaux," she responded in broken English.

Then Miles noticed one person in particular had not come in. He was especially curious. "So, where is my worthy opponent on the motorcycle? Where is the red knight? And the woman in black? I really need to be thanking her."

Everyone in the room looked at each other confused. Cas looked at him curiously as well. "Red knight? Woman in black? We don't know what you are referring to."

Miles stared at his elderly son blankly. How could he not know who they were? The red knight had even followed him into the rook. He shot a glance over at Chen. "Well, he knew who she was! Chen, tell him what happened on the way over here."

Chen laughed as he usually did and said, "I don't know

what you mean, Mr. Miles. I only see you at airport."

Miles was struck numb. *"Huh??"* he asked flummoxed. "You picked me up by the ocean in the middle of nowhere." Chen shook his head in confusion. "I don't get this. Cas, I thought she was part of your game." Cas looked on with concern and bewilderment. Then he turned to the eight kids and the two young men he flew against. "Well I know all you kids saw the woman in the mask. All of you ran like hell!"

All the teens traded frightened looks and began staring at the floor and whispering, "*Wiyyân, wiyyân.*"

Cas tilted his head slightly and looked on with great concern, along with the other adults in the room. "No one said anything about this…"

Suddenly, another door flew open on the other side of the room. A woman close to Cas' age came bursting through with a distraught look on her face.

"What's going on here?" she demanded. "What are all you kids doing here at this hour? Cas, tell me you didn't do what I think you…" Her eyes spotted Miles in the center of the room and her mouth fell open. She grasped her face and looked on as if she were horrified.

Miles did not understand. "I'm sorry, Miss. Are…are you alright?"

When she heard his voice, her eyes grew wider. "Oh no, Cas. Tell me you *didn't*. I warned you about this." Her hands fell to her sides and tears rolled down her cheeks.

A light went on in Miles' mind and he began to approach her. "Wait. I know your face."

"Oh, sweet merciful Heavens," she exclaimed. "You *did*, didn't you?"

Miles stood before the trembling woman. "Please don't be upset. It's really alright, I promise. I would know your beautiful face anywhere."

Her voice cracking and her hands shaking, she placed one on the side of his face and whispered, "Hello, Daddy." She collapsed in his arms and sobbed uncontrollably.

Miles held her tightly and closed his eyes. He was on the verge of losing control of his emotions as well. He could not believe all of this was real. "Hello Vivian, my sweet little lady." He smiled like a proud father. "Let me look at you. Look how beautiful you are."

She looked up at him, still in disbelief. Her eyes wet with tears. "I'm not little anymore, Daddy. And I'm not beautiful. I'm an *old* woman. And you. Look at *you*. You haven't aged a day." She pulled away from him and became furious again. "Cas, I told you about this. The *consequences*. Mother will *never* understand this."

Cas rebuked her. "Yes, she will. More than any of us. You are just not accepting of it."

"You're not *God*, Casden!" she shouted at him. "You have

no right to go messing around with the natural order of things. I won't be a party to this!"

"Stop it, both of you," Miles interjected. "You're both twice my age now, but you're still acting like kids." Vivian looked away from her brother with disdain. Miles walked in between his two children. "There must be a reason for this, just like you said earlier. Now tell me, where is your mother? Can one of you please tell me that? I mean, I'm here now aren't I? There's no changing that now. I just would like to see her please."

Cas looked over at his sister, allowing her to answer first since she was the oldest. Vivian sniffed her nose and cleared her throat. She looked more calmly at her father and answered him, "She's in the next room. I'll take you to her." She turned towards the rest of the family in the room and instructed them, "All of you get back home." The young kids groaned in protest. "No, no. Off you go. Fun time is over. Leave us be for now." Begrudgingly, one by one, they left the room, leaving Cas and Vivian alone with their father.

Miles smiled at them as they left. When the door closed, he looked over at Vivian and asked, "It's really you, isn't it honey? Look at you. You always took after Mom. People always said that of you." Vivian stood shaking as her father spoke. His voice began to crack with emotion but he tried to hold it in check. "I'm so proud of you both."

"I can't believe it's you," she said trembling. "I never believed any of it all this time. I didn't want to believe it. But now I…" She could not finish her thought. She was still too overcome with emotion.

"It's okay, Viv. It's not easy for me to grasp either." Miles cleared his throat. "Let's put that aside for now. Agreed?" She nodded in agreement. "Alright honey, please lead the way." Cas sat back down at the dinner table and looked on with a look of concern as Vivian led Miles to see his wife.

She placed her hand on the doorknob and then looked soulfully up at her dad. She did not have to say anything as he knew what she was thinking.

"It's okay." He nodded for her to go on in.

The room was partially lit. It was a large and expansive bedroom, decorated more ornately than the previous chamber. It even had a fireplace opposite the large bed. The embers were still smoldering inside. He found it odd that there was a need for a fireplace even though it was a tropical location. Then he remembered how elderly people can get cold easily and it began to make sense. On a bedside table, the first thing Miles noticed was the time on the digital clock. It was just past five in the morning. Even though there was a clock on the table, he could hear the tick-tock of another clock hanging on the wall. He noticed that it was an old German-style cuckoo clock. Finally, he slowly approached the bed behind his daughter. She turned on the bedside lamp.

There she was lying under a thin layer of covers. He could see the small frame of his wife's elderly body outlined in the covers. Her long, gray hair sprawled on the pillow. Her face was aged and sagging, but even though she was sixty years older, it was unmistakable to Miles who she was. He knew it was Vicky and his heart swelled in his chest when he finally laid eyes on her.

"Mama," Vivian said softly to her. Slowly her eyes opened and she looked at her daughter. Tears welled up inside Vivian's eyes as she knew her mother was waking. "Mama. I've brought someone to see you."

Miles knelt next to the bed and put his hand on top of his wife's. "Hello, my love," he whispered.

Vicky turned her head slightly and looked at him curiously. "I'm dreaming," she finally said. She looked up at Vivian and she shook her head.

"No, Mama."

She took a deep breath and then focused on Miles once more. Finally, as if a light had gone on in her mind, she smiled at him and squeezed his hand. "There's my handsome man." She touched his face and he took her hand and kissed the top of it as he had done a thousand times before. "I knew you would come." She tried to sit up. "Help me up." He immediately fixed a pillow behind her so she could sit up. He helped her slide towards the pillow so she was more upright. When she was comfortable, she reached for her glasses and Vivian instinctively handed them to her.

"Here, Mama," Vivian said.

She put her glasses on and then smiled again. "It really *is* you." Then she realized how she must look to him. "Oh my. I didn't have time to put on my face. How wretched I must look. An old lady lying in her nightgown. I wanted to look nicer when you arrived. I…I just couldn't stay awake."

"Oh honey," Miles smiled at her, "You're beautiful just the way you are."

Vicky coughed and chuckled as she did and responded, "You're my husband, alright. Only you could say something like that to an old woman like me. Sweet of you to say but I know damn well I look every bit of ninety-three years old." She looked at him closer and smiled. "Just look at you. Just as young and handsome as you always were. I knew what I was doing when I said yes to you."

"I was the lucky one, baby," he said lovingly. He still could not believe he was seeing her at this age. "But Victoria, I don't understand all this. Seeing you here. Our kids. How can all this be happening? *Why* could it be happening?"

"Cas knew he could find you and bring you here," she answered. "No one believed he could but I did. I believed in my boy. If he could rebuild cities and all those other things, I knew he could find his father."

"Find me? How was I lost?" Then it began to dawn on Miles. He did not know how but it was obvious he was never part of this time. "Oh Vicky." He sat on the bed next to her and held her hand. "I just realized. I'm not here am I? I mean the old me. You're…you're a widow?" Vicky looked at him with an obvious expression. "Oh my. Vicky, I'm so sorry." It was not every day that you find out that you were going to die before your spouse. The thought weighed on him heavily but he knew it must have been awful for his wife and his children. Now he understood Vivian's objections. He looked over at her. She was still standing behind him. Her arms were folded and her face expressionless. "Vivian, I'm sorry. I didn't understand until now."

"You have no idea," Vivian sneered. "It's like seeing a ghost. It's not right."

Miles stood up and tried to comfort her. "I know. It's not right. I understand how this could be so painful for you."

"No, you don't understand!"

"Vivian, please!" her mother scolded. "I would not have allowed this had I not approved. I gave Cas the permission to try it. It was my decision. I know you think I am selfish, but I felt it was necessary." Her voice began to shake and emotion overcame her. "I needed to see him one last time."

Vivian collapsed in her father's arms again and sobbed.

"I'm sorry, Mama. I'm sorry, Daddy."

He consoled her as best he could. "It's okay, honey. Think of this as a gift. I'm seeing things past my time. Things that I shouldn't see, but nevertheless I am. So, I'm going to embrace it. I'm going to embrace you as much as I can. That's the most precious thing to me. I don't want to throw that away."

"There is someone else who needed to see him, too," Vicky finally said.

Miles turned and looked at her curiously. He only needed a second to understand. He nodded in recognition. "Yes. You're right. There is isn't there?"

"No, Mama," Vivian pleaded. "It will kill her."

"Oh, no it won't. Trust me."

At that moment, the door to the bedroom opened. In walked a woman just a few years younger than Vivian. She had dark hair just as her mother once had, and was dressed in a traditional Thai gown. She stood in the middle of the floor and stared at Miles. Miles simply grinned at her from ear to-ear. She slowly walked towards him and stopped inches away. She examined his face with her hands ever so slowly. Tears rolled down Vicky's eyes as she watched. Vivian could not control herself as well. Cas came and stood in the doorway and looked on. The woman tilted her head just slightly as her eyes stayed on Miles. Then she smiled at him and said, "This is my daddy."

Miles was speechless. No words could describe what he

was feeling. Tears streamed down his cheeks. "I was hoping that was you dining with us."

"I wanted to keep you in suspense," Cas replied with slight grin.

"Hello there," he said softly and sweetly. "You must be my little girl." He wrapped his arms around her and held her tight.

"My name is Milena, as you know," she said softly. "But most people just call me Miley."

Miles chuckled. "You're named after me! I like that. You both had me going though. He said you were his sister-in-law."

Vivian was just as stunned to learn Miley had already seen their father. "Oh yes, Cas never gets tired of a good surprise."

Miley chuckled a bit as she continued to hold her father.

"What's so funny?" Miles asked.

"You called me 'ma'am.'" They both laughed even harder. Vicky smiled happily as she watched her children around their father.

He looked around the room at everyone. Vicky was thinking the same thing that he was. "How lucky, am I? I'm here with my family. And you're all so grown up. You have your own kids now, your own families. I'm so proud."

Miley produced a photo and showed it to him. He stared at it for a moment and he recognized it instantly. It was a photo of him and Vicky standing together in the French Quarter at night in front of St. Louis Cathedral. "Hey I remember this. We just took this. It was the last night before…" Then all-of-a-sudden his blood ran cold. He looked at Miley and asked, "You kept this picture all these years? Why?"

"It's my favorite picture of you and Mom," she answered. "She was pregnant with me. That's why it was my favorite." Then she said what he was afraid she was going to say. "I kept it so I would always know what you looked like."

Miles hands began to shake. He grew more nervous than ever before. "What I looked like? You mean you've never… seen me?" Miley shook her head as tears rolled down her cheeks. The inevitable was about to be exposed. His mind raced. Vicky sat on the bed looking on helplessly as Miles put all the pieces together. His eyes darted over towards Cas in a panic. Then to Vivian. "I taught you how to play chess when you were three. Then Cas said he had never played chess with me until now. If I'd never taught him chess before and Miley has never seen me, then that means I…"

Miles fell to his knees in shock. His wife and children looked on mournfully and sympathetically. There was nothing they could do. Cas bowed his head and walked out of the room and went to sit back down at the table. Miles crumbled to the floor in a heap. His whole life went before his eyes. Every moment in the past and every moment in the future. *"Why?"* he finally asked. "Why did you bring me here?"

Vicky slid her legs to the side of the bed. She struggled to get to her feet. Vivian offered to help her stand but Vicky waved her off and stood on her own. Vivian instead gave her a robe to keep warm. She slowly limped towards her stricken husband.

"The children and grandchildren all knew the tales about the great Miles Devereaux. They knew about your zest for life. How you loved your family and how you loved every day of your life." Miles looked at her still with a stunned expression. "You lived every day of your life like it was an adventure. And they wanted to give you one last great adventure!"

"You're speaking to me like I am *dead*," Miles protested.

"I am so sorry, my beloved," Vicky continued. "But you said it yourself. This is a gift!" Miles stood up and held her hand. She held on to him for support. "Embrace it just like you have embraced our children here tonight. There is nothing we can do about the past. But you can take this gift and live the adventure as if it were your last!"

"It is my last, isn't it?" Miles shook his head stepping away. His chest felt hollow. He could no longer feel anything at all. He did not know what to do. He felt like running but where would he go? It was all too much for him to take. "No!" he shouted. "I don't want this. I don't want to *die*. I must see our kids grow up. Take them to soccer games and Saints games. I want to be there for all the hurts and all the joys. All the first dates, graduations, weddings. I *can't* die at such a young age." His mind ached and his body felt like it had been zapped with thousands of volts of electricity.

Vicky limped towards him and placed her hand on his shoulder and said the inevitable. "Yes, you can."

It was too much for Vivian. She ran out of the room in tears. But not Miley. She kept looking at her father. She knew this was a rare moment for her. She did not want to miss a second of being in his presence.

"Wait," Miles said holding his hands up. "Wait a minute. I can fix this."

"There is nothing you can do, my love," Vicky insisted. "You don't belong here. You…we were given this only chance."

"I can fix this!" He bolted out of the room and walked straight towards Cas. "How does it work? I demand to know."

Miley and her mother followed him out into the open chamber. Vicky slowly made her way to one of the sofas. Cas looked up at his father sorrowfully. "You can only know what one learns on his own."

"Don't talk to me in riddles, Casden," Miles yelled. "Now, please tell me. How does time travel work?"

Cas sat silently. He knew what his father wanted to do, but he knew it would never work.

"It's nearly dawn," Vivian stated. "He doesn't have much time. Tell him."

"Tell him, Cas," his mother insisted. "Tell him before it's too late." Cas still sat defiantly quiet.

"Too late for what? What happens at dawn?" Miles yelped. Then he tried to reason with them. "I don't want to leave. If I'm going to die in the past, then why can't I just stay here? All of you are here." He ran over to Vicky and knelt beside her. "I just want to be with you honey. With you, my wife. And all of our kids."

Vicky looked at him sympathetically. "Miles, my dearest one. You know there is nothing I've wanted more in this world than for you to be here with me and all of us. But it's not possible."

"Why isn't it?" he sobbed.

Miley came and touched him on the shoulder. "Because it only works for one night, Daddy. Cas can tell you."

Miles stumbled to his feet. "One night only? One night to see my family? One night to see my second daughter for the only time? One night in...in *Bangkok* of all places?" He threw his hands up in exasperation and shook his weary head in sadness. Then he remembered his only hope. "I can fix this. You can just send me back early, right? How does it work? Please Cas!"

"Tell him, Cas!" Vivian cried. Cas remained silent.

Miley finally said it for him. "It's the marbles."

Miles was dumbfounded. "The *what?*"

Cas looked up at him finally and plainly answered, "Check your pocket."

When Miles looked down, he was no longer wearing the traditional Thai robes he was given after his shower. He was wearing the same clothes he had on when he awakened on the plane. Stunned, he started searching his pockets as everyone in the room witnessed his instant transformation. Shocked and amazed as they were, no one said anything. They watched as he desperately searched. He felt frantically and searched everywhere on his clothing until his hand froze on his breast pocket. He slipped his fingers inside and to his amazement he produced a single marble. He held it in his fingers and raised it close to his eyes. It was brilliantly clear and translucent. Intertwined in the middle of the ball were bands of glittery gold and silver that sparkled in the light. His eyes widened. He had never seen a marble so dazzling in color and decadence.

"The Lutz marble," Cas said casually. He rose from his chair as did Vicky from the couch. She craned her neck to get a better look at the stunning marble. Cas walked directly up to Miles. "Designed and created by Nicolas Lutz sometime in the late nineteenth century. He continued to create them until just after 1900 and then he abruptly stopped. They were prized by collectors around the world for their glittery appearance and for their meticulous design inside and out. They were prized by some but priceless to others." Miles stood wide-eyed as he listened to his son describe the tiny, glassy ball. "But a marble is just a child's toy. *This* is no toy. No. This is something like no other. *This* is an incandescent globule, or simply, an orb. It seems simplistic at first glance, but when you look deep inside the orb, its appearance is almost...otherworldly." Miles raised the orb closer to his eyes. Inside was a brilliance he had never seen before. The bands of glitter seemed to come alive as he looked deeper, as if an entire galaxy of worlds were inside the tiny globe. It was a whole other world of beauty. There were bands of stars surrounding galaxies and inside those galaxies were more bands of stars surrounding even more galaxies. It was like nothing he had ever dreamed before.

Miles snapped to attention as Cas continued to explain the Lutz orb. "Sometime in the early to mid-twentieth century, an unknown collector began going around the world searching for every such marble created by Lutz in hopes he would find in them these special incandescent orbs."

Miles took his eyes off the marble and looked at Cas and asked, "Why? I mean, how would he know?"

Cas continued, "The man secretly learned that some of the marbles were not just ordinary ones as you can see. He found that they contained within the bands a certain unknown element. Something that made the ribbon bands sparkle with thousands of tiny flashes of light each time the ball bounced or rolled. He then learned about its most hidden secret." Everyone in the room looked on in anticipation. "Whenever he had one in his possession, he could think of a place and instantly travel there. *Then* he found he could even travel to other points in time." Miles could not believe what he was hearing. Yet he stared at the tiny ball in his hand and knew that Cas must be telling the truth. "You see, inside the orb, *this is time.*"

"This is stunning! What happened to the man?" Miles asked curiously.

Vicky grasped onto a cane that was leaning against the couch and she slowly walked over to them. "No one knows. He disappeared. But his collection was left behind, hidden in a closet in an old building on Canal Street. Until it was discovered."

Miles could not believe his ears. When he heard the street name, his jaw dropped. "I know you're not going to say in our building in New Orleans."

"That's precisely what I'm saying," Vicky assured him. "Right in our house."

"*Good Lord,*" Miles gasped. "Discovered by who?"

"By me," Cas answered. "But I didn't know what I had found or what they could do until years later."

Miles took a deep breath and stared at the orb and then back at Cas. "Let me guess. You found them when you were about one year old. And I'm guessing sometime before the same night..."

"As the hurricane," Vivian said completing his thought.

"Sweet Jesus," Miles gasped. He knew right then and there that what they were telling him was true. All of it. He studied the orb even closer. He knew this was the answer. He knew this was his only way back to try and change the past. "This little thing? This...this incandescent...*ball?* I didn't' even know I still had it on me." He thought back again to the night of the hurricane. "Wait a minute." He thought even harder. "You were rolling them down the hall. And then I dove to catch one before I..." He froze. For a moment, he had a vision. It was a vision of himself, a vision of himself screaming *'No!'* He shook his head, trying to shake it off. "Oh man. This is beyond wild." It was all so much that his mind could barely handle it. He studied the marble once more. "So, all I need is this and I can go back?"

Cas took the orb from him. "No. This one will no longer work. Once it is used to travel through time, its power is diminished and all that one can do is teleport within time. Soon, that ability is lost as well."

Miles chuckled out loud. "Now that. The teleporting is *very* cool." He thought for a moment. "And my clothes changing? That, too?"

Cas and Vivian nodded. Miley laughed and answered,

"Pretty nifty, huh?"

Then he snapped to reality once again and began to panic. "Wait a minute. It's been used already. You mean...it won't work anymore? You mean I'm stuck here?"

"Not unless..." Cas answered as he walked over to a small cabinet fixed inside the wall. He opened it with a key he produced from his robe. The door opened and revealed a small glass bowl full of the dazzling orbs. "You have another."

"Oh, thank *God!*" Miles sighed as he wiped his forehead.

Cas stared at the bowl with a terrible look of concern. Vicky could sense his troubles as well. Miles looked on with suspicion.

"What is it?" Miles asked.

"You mentioned something that troubles me," Cas finally said. "And what the young ones were saying earlier: *Wiyyân*."

"What? What is *wiyyân*?"

"The red knight and this woman you saw. She was wearing this...what was it? A black mask?" Miles nodded attentively. Cas certainly had his attention. He had a feeling Cas knew more about them than what he let on. "Vivian is right when she speaks of consequences. What these tiny round pieces of glass can do is marvelous and extraordinarily mysterious. But with them comes a warning." Miles gulped. "In the Thai culture, there are many superstitions; among them is the fear and the belief in spirits or ghosts, or as what they were saying, '*wiyyân*.'

There are many spirits for countless different places or situations. Time is not meant to be disturbed and when it is there are guardians to watch over such disturbances. There are guardians of good but also of evil and they will stop at nothing to see to it that any disturbance in the natural order of time is either punished or stamped out."

"What about the good ones?" He remembered how helpful the woman in black was during the game. He could not believe she could be evil.

"The good are there to set things right despite the disturbance in time. Even though this disturbance has happened, it is their duty to get things back as they were. Albeit in their own way."

Miles looked at him suspiciously. How did he know so much about all this? "Are you saying this red knight is really after me? She really wasn't part of the game?"

Cas cleared his throat. "What I had planned for you was indeed a game, but she was never part of it. She inserted herself into it I'm afraid." He picked one orb from the bowl and handed it to Miles. "That is why you must hurry. Your only chance is to use this new one before dawn."

Miley rushed over. "He needs to be outside or it won't be accurate." She began to lead him quickly to the door.

Miles held up his hands to stop her. "Whoa, wait a minute! What do you mean accurate? How will I know I'm going back to the right time? And why outside? I was in a hallway when…"

Cas cut him off. "It's what is in your mind. If you are focused on that time, that is where you will go. If you are unaware or taken by surprise, then the focus of time must be redirected by another source. That is how you arrived here. I was able to give direction for you."

"You've got to be kidding!" Miles shrieked. "You were only one. How do you know all this?"

"There is no time to explain. We must hurry!"

Miles would not move. He still looked at his son with suspicion. "Cas…" he began. "You've tried this? You've done this before?" Cas was silent. "You said it was years before you knew what these things could do." Miles froze and stared into the unknown, racing to try and figure everything out at once. "Oh geez…you *have* done this before, haven't you? How else could you have directed me here from 2005?" Casden looked at him as if he were guilty of a crime. There was no need for him to respond. Miles already knew the answer.

Vicky looked at the clock and panicked. "The sun is coming Casden! He has less than twenty-five minutes if that."

"But I need to tell all of you goodbye!" Miles cried. "Don't rush me like this! Victoria!" He slipped from Vivian's hand and ran to his wife.

"No goodbyes, my dearest," Vicky said, her voice shaking. "I never got one before." Miles looked at her sorrowfully. He could not imagine the pain she must have suffered all these years. "But Miles my dearest, my love for you is the same." She leaned in and whispered into his ear. "It is eternal."

Miles wanted to cry right then and there but everything was happening too fast. All he could do was feel for them.

"Daddy," Miley said. "Love is not bound by time. We are your family." She pulled the amulet from under his collar and squeezed it in her hand as she kissed his cheek. "Keep us with you."

He looked at his daughter lovingly, not knowing the significance of her gesture, but he knew that she meant it in the most powerful way. He gazed upon her and Vicky one last time before Cas and Vivian whisked him away.

They rushed him out of the room and to a rounded stairway. They quickly climbed the stairs in the high corridor and stopped at the doorway at the center. Cas and Vivian glanced at one another. Miles could tell there was a look of uncertainty on both their faces.

"Remember," Cas began, "focus on the time you wish to travel. Block everything else out." He opened the door and pushed Miles outside. He stumbled out onto the roof of the expansive home.

Vivian looked increasingly worried. "What if she is there?" she hissed to her brother so Miles would not hear.

"We must protect him until he is away! You know this!" Cas fired back.

The three of them walked to the center of the roof. There was a clear view of the night skyline of Bangkok. Miles stood and looked at it with wonder. *Will I ever see such a sight again?* he thought to himself.

"Do you have the orb? Show it to me!" Cas commanded. Miles complied and showed him the unused incandescent orb. "Hold it tightly in your hand and focus!"

He looked over at Vivian and smiled at her. He wanted to say something to her but all he could do is look at her as a proud father would do. She understood immediately what he was feeling and thinking.

"I'll see you in New Orleans," she said smiling. "Just a tad bit younger I imagine."

Miles smiled broadly and caressed the side of her face as he had always done with her. He looked over at Cas and all he could do was look at his son with admiration and pride. No words had to be said. His son knew what his father's gaze meant. Miles simply tapped his hand lightly on Cas' shoulder and nodded. Cas smiled at him in return.

But then at the last moment, Cas broke the silence between them. "Hey, Pop. Great game."

Miles smiled at him and answered, "You bet."

He stepped away from them and looked straight up into

the Heavens. He took one last deep breath and then he closed his eyes.

Keith R. Rees

Chapter 8
Checkmate

Miley stood in the chamber with her elderly mother, staring at the door to the stairwell. Her hands shook as tears welled in her eyes. Vicky was too weak to stand any longer. She sat on the cushioned chair at the dining table and took a deep breath.

"Go to him, Miley," she said. "Go and see him one last time."

Miley hesitated and looked over her shoulder and answered, "None of this is right. Something is not right. I can feel it."

Vicky nodded in agreement, saying, "Yes. As can I. Go, go!"

Miley stood and trembled even more as a feeling of dread overwhelmed her. It was then she realized what was about to happen. "Oh, my *God*..."

"*Go*, Miley," Vicky cried.

In an instant, Miley burst through the door and went running up the rounded staircase as fast as she could. She reached the top and turned the handle on the rooftop door and slammed her weight into it. Stumbling out onto the roof, she emerged to see her father standing in the center with his eyes closed and fists clinched.

Vivian and Cas looked over at her as they heard her crashing through the door and yelled in unison, "*Miley*,"

Miley screamed out, "*Daddy*. Look *out*."

"*No*," Cas yelled.

But it was too late. As soon as he heard his daughter's voice, Miles opened his eyes. Instead of seeing his home in 2005 New Orleans, he still saw the future. He also saw a flash of fiery red coming straight towards him.

His three children gasped in horror as a trail of fiery red careened straight into Miles, lifting him from his feet. Miles felt a piercing thud to his mid-section and a rush of wind as he felt himself lifted and tossed through the air. The force of the blow sent him sailing towards the edge of the roof.

Instinctively, Cas reached inside his robe, pulled out a small device, and tossed it like a Frisbee with lightning-quick speed. "Catch this, Father!"

Although stunned by the sheer magnitude of what hit

him, Miles heard his son's cry. He held his hands up to his chest as the object sailed towards him. He caught it like a tight-end in mid-air as he sailed over the edge of the roof.

"Squeeze it, Daddy!" Vivian screamed at the top of her lungs.

Miles went flying off the roof and towards the ground. The last thing he could recall was the screaming voice of his daughter. He grasped the object in his hands and squeezed with all his might as he fell. Instantly a sphere chaser encased him inside and stopped his freefall. The transparent sphere floated in mid-air with Miles sprawled across the bottom. Once again, he was dressed in the sleek black uniform with majestic purple stripe down the side. His shoes were gravity gliders as well. He tried to gather his senses and get to his feet. As he floated away from the house, he could see his children standing on the edge of the roof looking down with relief. Then, something else caught his eye. A streak of fiery red trailed off in the distance.

"The red knight," Miles shrieked. "Cas, you weren't kidding." Miles locked his feet in place and instantly the seat and the controls appeared before him. He immediately took off towards the trail of the red knight. "I'm going after her," he yelled as he passed over his kids.

"There's no *time*," Cas yelled back.

Suddenly, the face of Gigi appeared on the inside walls of the sphere chaser. Miles was stunned to see her. "*You* again,"

Cas saw her appear as well as Miles sped away in the chaser. "*Gigi*," He pulled his sleeve up to reveal his Comm-Vice. "GG 42-7, I command you to disable." But nothing happened. Miles sped away towards the city after the red knight. Cas immediately headed for the door back inside. "I'm going after them."

"No," Miley insisted, "let me go. I'm better in a chaser than you are." Cas relented and let her go ahead of him. She raced down the stairs to fetch another activator.

Miles accelerated the sphere chaser to its top speed. As he kept his eyes fixed on the red knight's trail, he shot a glance over at Gigi. "What do you want? I don't believe this is a coincidence!"

"Where do you belong, Miles?" Gigi asked coyly.

"Don't play games with me. *Up yours!* You got *that* in your sub-routines?"

He watched as the red knight landed on the top of one of the skyscrapers in downtown Bangkok. The eastern sky began to glow as the sunrise came fast approaching. Miles landed the chaser steadily on the roof. The sphere closed instantly as he stepped out. The red knight stood on the other side, still wearing the darkened helmet.

"How did you fly like that without a sphere chaser?" Miles asked loudly. "Show me your face, Gigi!"

The red knight removed her helmet. It was indeed Gigi

inside the fiery red suit. "Where do you belong, Miles?" she asked again.

"I *knew* it," Miles exclaimed. "I belong at home, with my family. That's where I am going, and you're not going to stop me."

Gigi tossed the helmet aside and unsheathed a *krabi*. She pointed it towards him. "This is not your home. You do not belong. Now you will not belong anywhere."

She began to advance on him. He looked around quickly but did not see anything to use as a weapon. He did remember one thing; he now knew how to fight. He assumed the stance for the *Muay-Thai*. Gigi swished the sword at him but he effortlessly ducked away. He moved like a stealth expert on his toes as he dodged her every move. She was fast and deft and wielded the *krabi* like a seasoned veteran. He wondered if she was still a hologram. There was only one way to find out. He looked for an opening as he kept defying her every attack with the sword. As she threw another thrust towards him, he slid under and quickly threw a roundhouse kick and landed it perfectly on her jaw. She was real alright. She stumbled backwards from the force of the blow. Miles smiled with satisfaction.

"What happened?" he asked sarcastically. "Not holographic anymore, are you?" Gigi rubbed her jaw with the side of her hand. "Stings, doesn't it?" They began battling again.

High in the air came another sphere chaser. Miley hovered above the rooftop watching the action below. She wanted to land and help Miles but she knew she could not keep up. She could not risk getting hurt by Gigi either. She looked on helplessly.

Miles matched Gigi's every move. Not once could she land a blow with the sword. In frustration, she threw the *krabi* to the side and took the stance of the *Muay-Thai*.

"You taught me well, Gigi. But why? Why did you teach me?"

They began to fight hand to hand *Muay-Thai*. They fought and moved like masters all across the landscape of the roof. Arms swished and flashed as they danced lightly on their toes. Kicks flew and heads dodged. They put on an artistic display of elegance and deadly force. They were masters and equals in every move and neither could gain the upper hand in the epic battle.

As they traded kicks and punches, Miles tried to understand why all this was happening. Why did Gigi keep insisting that he did not belong? And why was she now fighting so hard to keep him from leaving?

"You put me through challenges. Then you taught me to fight!" He repelled more of her kicks and punches as he spoke. "Now you say I don't belong!"

"You wanted adventure," Gigi responded.

Miles looked at her slanted. "But I didn't choose this adventure."

"You still broke the rules of time."

"It wasn't my doing!" he insisted. "It was thrust upon me."

"Nevertheless," Gigi replied as she finally landed a perfect roundhouse to his head. He went flailing backwards and landed on his back. The tiny incandescent orb fell from his pocket unbeknownst to him. "We cannot allow it." Gigi smiled fiendishly as Miles lay sprawled out on the roof. "Check."

Miles shook his head in a daze. "We?"

He sat up and whipped his head around to see the woman in black standing on the edge of the roof. Her long black cape swirled in the wind high above the sparkling city. The symbol of infinity glistened on the side of her arm. The glow of the sunrise began to brighten behind her.

"You're the guardians," Miles whispered.

Miley was stunned. She had never seen the woman in black before. She was speechless.

The woman in black glared at Gigi, and she glared back. Miles sat and watched in shock as Gigi threw her hands toward the woman in black and sent an invisible force towards her, knocking her from the ledge.

"You wanted to know how I can fly without using a sphere chaser?" she asked sarcastically. "It's simple. Time flies!" In a flash of speed, Gigi raced towards Miles as he hurtled away on his back. The awesome power shocked him. Before he knew it, she darted away into the air. He and Miley were astonished as they watched her sail off into the sky.

He got to his feet and suddenly found himself alone. He looked at the sky and knew it was almost sunrise. Miley landed her sphere on the roof.

"Now's my chance," he said out loud.

"Yes," Miley yelled back. "You must hurry, they are gone." She ran and stood by him and looked at him eerily. "By the way, where did you learn to move like that? That was amazing. She couldn't lay a finger on you."

"Ha, you got me. Might wanna ask your brother that one. Stand back!"

Miles walked to the center of the rooftop and then he reached inside his shirt pocket. There was nothing there. He patted himself on the other pocket, then in desperation on his pants pockets. He searched everywhere. The orb was nowhere to be found!

"Oh, *shit!* She took it!" He began to panic. He looked all around the roof and across the sky. "I don't believe this." Then he remembered his sphere chaser. He ran towards the activator sitting on the roof. He picked it up and quickly squeezed it. Immediately he was encased.

"How will you find her?" Miley called out.

"I don't know. I'm making this up as I go along." He took

off into the glowing sky of the oncoming sunrise. He was right about one thing. He had no idea how to find Gigi.

Suddenly, Gigi once again appeared on the transparent wall of his sphere chaser. "Checkmate, Miles. You lose."

"I don't think so! Give it back to me!"

"You'll never find me," she answered smartly.

Miles thought quickly about his options. "Then I'll just go back to Cas' place and get another one."

"It doesn't work that way, Miles. You must use this one. And besides, you'll never make it in time." She disappeared from the screen. Miles repeated in his mind what she had just said. 'Never make it in time. Never make it in time.' *In time.* Then he understood. She was a guardian of time. She was all about time. She *was* time. However, she did have a counterpart.

Out of the corner of his eye he saw her. The woman in black was standing on the ledge of another high building. Miles raced towards her. As soon as he reached her she was gone again. Miles slowed and looked around. He panicked for a moment. Then he saw her again. She stood much further away on another spire atop a building. Miles nodded in comprehension and sped towards her.

"That's it. Show me the way," he muttered.

He followed her through the city's immense skyline. Gravity gliders zipped by on the ground and up and down the sides of the glass buildings. He had thought he would never see it again moments before on the roof of Cas' house. But, here he was, witnessing the marvels of man and what would happen sixty years from his time. His sphere chaser reflected in the glass of the buildings as he passed between them. What an adventure he was on. He had seen his family in the future. He got to meet them. Dine with them. Touch and hold them. All in this time. It was a concept he still could not fully grasp. As he followed the woman in black through the skyline maze, he thought of what he learned of his own fate. That he would actually die before his third child would even be born. *How? And when?* What could he be going back to? He did not know the answers to any of those questions, but what he did know was Gigi and Victoria were both right. He truly did not belong there.

He banked right and then he saw the woman in black once again. He recognized where he was heading as she perched at the very top of the Giant Swing. Then he saw Gigi. She was standing in the middle of the square in front of the temple. Miles landed the sphere chaser with a dazzling roll. The sphere collapsed and he skidded to a stop on glider shoes. He turned and glared at Gigi, who was smiling, as if she shared none of his urgency in the situation.

On the other side of the square, Miley landed her sphere chaser and watched as Miles faced Gigi again. She noticed that Gigi was armed with the *Krabi-krabong*.

"Dad!" she yelled. "Think fast!" She produced a set of *Krabi-krabong* from her chaser and flung them towards Miles. He caught them perfectly.

He smiled appreciatively at her. "*That's* my girl."

"Hello, Miles," Gigi said casually. To his surprise, she instantly transformed into Chen. He was dressed in the same chauffeur's uniform and hat just like he was before. Both Miley and Miles' eyes widened.

"Hello, Mr. Miles," he said again.

Miles was beside himself. "That's some trick, Gigi. No wonder Chen had no idea about the pickup at the beach. It was *you* the whole time." Chen paced a few steps back and forth. He pitched the orb up and down in his hand, smiling and chuckling the entire time. "I don't know what your deal is but I need that back. I don't have much time."

Chen instantly transformed back into Gigi as she continued to toss the orb into the air. "It's funny you should say that, Miles. My deal *is* time because I *am* time. I'm *not* one to be trifled with."

"Neither am *I*."

They both lunged at one another and began fighting with their weapons. They danced around the square like masters with swords swishing and clanging and clubs knocking together. The sounds of the battle echoed across the large and ancient square.

Miley's eyes were fixed on them. She could not believe what her father could do. She marveled as he whirled around on his toes, keeping perfect balance as he fought off each attack from Gigi.

"You may as well give up," Gigi said wryly. "You're never getting this orb."

"And you may as well bite me. I'm never giving up!"

As he thwarted another one of her charges, he hopped onto the first step of the pedestal of the Giant Swing. He shuffled his feet on the edge and kept her at bay. He knew the higher ground would give him the advantage.

Suddenly, the advantage worked. He knocked her club from her hands and she was down to just the sword. In two quick moves, he jabbed her with the club right on the lip as if he threw a punch like a prize fighter. She stumbled backwards as her lip began to show a little blood.

"Time can bleed, huh?" he mused out loud.

Gigi shrugged it off. "Just like your seconds are bleeding away."

Miles hopped down from the step. He knew he was losing time. She was absolutely right. He slashed his sword through the air, forcing her to back away.

Miley ran towards them. She could sense the urgency. "The sun is coming up, Gigi. You know that."

She casually answered, "Four minutes and thirty-three

seconds to be exact."

Miles glanced around the square in a panic. He looked atop the Giant Swing but the woman in black was nowhere to be seen. Gigi thrust her sword and Miles batted it away. The swords clanged together in three quick swipes.

"Maybe we could bargain," Miles suggested. "What do you want for it?"

Miley inched closer. "You have no right to do this. You were not created for this. Give it back to him."

"You think your brother created me? That senile old fool?" She glared at Miles. "You have nothing to give, Miles. And there is nothing I need."

On the other side of the large pedestal that the Giant Swing rested upon, an old homeless man began to stir. He heard voices arguing out in the square. He got to his feet and stumbled around the base of the structure to see who it was.

"What the hell is this?" the homeless man shouted. "Can't anyone get a moment's peace around here?"

Gigi, Miley, and Miles all looked over at the man with surprise. Miles recognized him immediately. It was the same old black man from the alley earlier in the night.

"Hey, I know you!" Miles cried out.

Gigi's eyes widened. Suddenly the man zipped from where he was standing right through her, making her disappear. Then in a flash the man was standing right in front of Miles.

"Holy crap," Miles exclaimed. "She *evaporated*."

"Oh, my *word*," Miley gasped.

"Nah. She just got out the way," the man said casually. "And she was in mine. She don't want any part of me."

Miles stood bewildered and puzzled. "I saw you earlier. The eagle man, right? You were the one dining on alley rats." The man let out a loud bellow of a laugh. "Who *are* you?"

The man lifted his tattered sleeve and revealed a tattoo of a perfectly etched symbol on his arm. "You're a mathematician, Miles. You tell me."

His eyes widened. "*Infinity*. That's the symbol for infinity. Just like the one I saw on the woman in black." Miles shook his head in amazement. "You mean you know who she is?"

"You could say that. It's our job to make sure time keeps movin' on. And time was startin' to get on my nerves."

Miley gasped again. She was stunned. "Good *Lord*."

Miles smiled and nodded in appreciation. "You're a guardian of time."

"Now you got it, man," the man laughed out loud again. "And now you got this, too." He held up the shiny incandescent orb between his fingers. Relief washed over Miles like a warm blanket. His daughter breathed a huge sigh of relief, too. "Think you might be needin' this…" He reached to hand the orb over to Miles when suddenly a gravity glider came racing across the square and plucked Miles right off his feet before he could grab the orb. The man watched in shock as Gigi raced away with Miles clinging to the side of the car.

"Ah, damnit," he snarled. The old black man instantly vanished and bolted towards the speeding gravity glider. Miley looked on in speechless horror.

Miles screamed out as he tried desperately to keep his balance on his gliders. Somehow his hands were fastened to the side of the car and he could not move them.

"You're not going anywhere, Miles," the voice of Gigi announced. He looked inside the window of the car and saw her face on the control screen.

Miles held on for dear life as the car raced around the streets of Bangkok. It went up and down highways, through alleyways, and then back to the skyscrapers and multi-level freeways. There were cars everywhere now that dawn approached. As they ascended yet another tall building, Miles maneuvered around on his gliders. He was able to lift his hands and move them as well. The wind lashed against him as the glider dragged him at terrific speed. He skated on the side of the glassy building as he held onto the car. As it reached the summit and leveled out, he freed his hands and leaped onto the top of the car.

High above came Miley in her sphere chaser. She watched the incredible scene down below with her father clinging to the side of the gravity glider.

Suddenly, another glider came racing up beside them and matched their speed. The eagle man was driving the glider and standing atop it was the woman in black. Miles looked at her wide-eyed and stunned. She pointed ahead of them. Miles looked to where she was pointing and saw that they were actually on a highway that was incomplete. The road was going to fall out from under them in a matter of seconds.

"Oh, my God, *no*," Miley shrieked as she put her hand over her mouth in terror.

"She's going to *kill* me," Miles shouted. He flattened himself on the roof and shouted towards the screen on the car. "Gigi, you can't do this!"

"I can, Miles," Gigi replied. The look on her face was somber as could be as the car accelerated towards the drop-off.

Miles watched as the edge of the expansive building approached. He looked on in horror as he knew he was about to fall to his death. He looked one last time over at the woman in black. She stood defiantly as her car approached the edge as well.

"We're goin' over!" he yelled at her. Out of the corner of his eye he saw her grin just slightly with a wink.

In an instant, both cars went sailing off the edge of the building and straight into the abyss towards the Earth. Miley gasped in horror as she watched them plummet off the edge. Miles could not think at all. As the cars fell from under them, the woman in black tossed the incandescent orb underhanded towards him. As if they were moving in slow motion, he became aware of the orb sailing through the air and landed directly in his outstretched hand.

"Use it for good," he heard her whisper. He caught it. As soon as it touched his hand the orb began to glow a brilliant sky blue. He immediately closed his fist around it. Not knowing what would happen next, or without even a hint of anything to focus on, all he could see was the amulet dangling around his neck as he descended. He remembered just then what Miley had told him. "We are your family."

The first break of sunlight came pouring over the horizon and shone upon the photo of the young girl with long black hair. It was the only picture in his mind when he closed his eyes. Miley closed hers, too.

The woman in black smiled. Her mission was accomplished. She closed her eyes as well and directed her focus on Miles. In a flash, he disappeared into thin air just before he reached the ground.

Keith R. Rees

Epilogue

As the sun began to rise over the city of Bangkok, the streets came alive. The essence of life rose from the streets of speeding gliders and the busy populace below. It rose past the mirrored spectacles, the endless columns of buildings that stood like majestic cathedrals, and past the astonishing skyways of the future. The immense majesty that was Bangkok sprawled towards the horizon in splendor as the coming of day commenced.

Watching over it all, standing upon the highest spire of the magnificent city, was the woman in black. The symbol of infinity on her arm was emblazoned in the morning sun. Her long, silky black hair cascaded down her shoulders and her long shimmering black cape swirled in the wind.

Keith R. Rees

About the Author

Keith R. Rees has been writing professionally for over 20 years. ONE NIGHT IN BANGKOK, a science fiction work, is the first installment in what is projected to become The One Night Trilogy. He has always been a fan of science fiction, particularly stories that involve time travel, and writes stories that have both realistic and human sides to them.

Author site at https://reeskeithr.wixsite.com/krrees

Keith R. Rees

If you enjoyed *One Night in Bangkok*, consider these other fine books from Savant Books and Publications:

Essay, Essay, Essay by Yasuo Kobachi
Aloha from Coffee Island by Walter Miyanari
Footprints, Smiles and Little White Lies by Daniel S. Janik
The Illustrated Middle Earth by Daniel S. Janik
Last and Final Harvest by Daniel S. Janik
A Whale's Tale by Daniel S. Janik
Tropic of California by R. Page Kaufman
Tropic of California (the companion music CD) by R. Page Kaufman
The Village Curtain by Tony Tame
Dare to Love in Oz by William Maltese
The Interzone by Tatsuyuki Kobayashi
Today I Am a Man by Larry Rodness
The Bahrain Conspiracy by Bentley Gates
Called Home by Gloria Schumann
Kanaka Blues by Mike Farris
First Breath edited by Z. M. Oliver
Poor Rich by Jean Blasiar
The Jumper Chronicles by W. C. Peever
William Maltese's Flicker by William Maltese
My Unborn Child by Orest Stocco
Last Song of the Whales by Four Arrows
Perilous Panacea by Ronald Klueh
Falling but Fulfilled by Zachary M. Oliver
Mythical Voyage by Robin Ymer
Hello, Norma Jean by Sue Dolleris
Richer by Jean Blasiar
Manifest Intent by Mike Farris
Charlie No Face by David B. Seaburn
Number One Bestseller by Brian Morley
My Two Wives and Three Husbands by S. Stanley Gordon
In Dire Straits by Jim Currie
Wretched Land by Mila Komarnisky
Chan Kim by Ilan Herman
Who's Killing All the Lawyers? by A. G. Hayes
Ammon's Horn by G. Amati
Wavelengths edited by Zachary M. Oliver
Almost Paradise by Laurie Hanan
Communion by Jean Blasiar and Jonathan Marcantoni
The Oil Man by Leon Puissegur

One Night in Bangkok

Random Views of Asia from the Mid-Pacific by William E. Sharp
The Isla Vista Crucible by Reilly Ridgell
Blood Money by Scott Mastro
In the Himalayan Nights by Anoop Chandola
On My Behalf by Helen Doan
Traveler's Rest by Jonathan Marcantoni
Keys in the River by Tendai Mwanaka
Chimney Bluffs by David B. Seaburn
The Loons by Sue Dolleris
Light Surfer by David Allan Williams
The Judas List by A. G. Hayes
Path of the Templar—Book 2 of The Jumper Chronicles by W. C. Peever
The Desperate Cycle by Tony Tame
Shutterbug by Buz Sawyer
Blessed are the Peacekeepers by Tom Donnelly and Mike Munger
The Bellwether Messages edited by D. S. Janik
The Turtle Dances by Daniel S. Janik
The Lazarus Conspiracies by Richard Rose
Purple Haze by George B. Hudson
Imminent Danger by A. G. Hayes
Lullaby Moon (CD) by Malia Elliott of Leon & Malia
Volutions edited by Suzanne Langford
In the Eyes of the Son by Hans Brinckmann
The Hanging of Dr. Hanson by Bentley Gates
Flight of Destiny by Francis Powell
Elaine of Corbenic by Tima Z. Newman
Ballerina Birdies by Marina Yamamoto
More More Time by David B. Seabird
Crazy Like Me by Erin Lee
Cleopatra Unconquered by Helen R. Davis
Valedictory by Daniel Scott
The Chemical Factor by A. G. Hayes
Quantum Death by A. G. Hayes and Raymond Gaynor
Big Heaven by Charlotte Hebert
Captain Riddle's Treasure by GV Rama Rao
All Things Await by Seth Clabough
Tsunami Libido by Cate Burns
Finding Kate by A. G. Hayes
The Adventures of Purple Head, Buddha Monkey and Sticky Feet by Erik and Forest Bracht
In the Shadows of My Mind by Andrew Massie
The Gumshoe by Richard Rose

Keith R. Rees

In Search of Somatic Therapy by Setsuko Tsuchiya
Cereus by Z. Roux
The Solar Triangle by A. G. Hayes
Shadow and Light edited by Helen R. Davis
A Real Daughter by Lynne McKelvey
StoryTeller by Nicholas Bylotas
Bo Henry at Three Forks by Daniel Bradford
Navel of the Sea by Elizabeth McKague

Coming Soon
Kindred edited by Gary "Doc" Krinberg

Savant Books and Publications
http://www.savantbooksandpublications.com

One Night in Bangkok

and from our *avant garde* imprint, Aignos Publishing:

The Dark Side of Sunshine by Paul Guzzo
Happy that it's Not True by Carlos Aleman
Cazadores de Libros Perdidos by German William Cabasssa Barber [Spanish]
The Desert and the City by Derek Bickerton
The Overnight Family Man by Paul Guzzo
There is No Cholera in Zimbabwe by Zachary M. Oliver
John Doe by Buz Sawyers
The Piano Tuner's Wife by Jean Yamasaki Toyama
Nuno by Carlos Aleman
An Aura of Greatness by Brendan P. Burns
Polonio Pass by Doc Krinberg
Iwana by Alvaro Leiva
University and King by Jeffrey Ryan Long
The Surreal Adventures of Dr. Mingus by Jesus Richard Felix Rodriguez
Letters by Buz Sawyers
In the Heart of the Country by Derek Bickerton
El Camino De Regreso by Maricruz Acuna [Spanish]
Diego in Two Places by Carlos Aleman
Prepositions by Jean Yamasaki Toyama
Deep Slumber of Dogs by Doc Krinberg
Saddam's Parrot by Jim Currie
Beneath Them by Natalie Roers
Chang the Magic Cat by A. G. Hayes
Illegal by E. M. Duesel
Island Wildlife: Exiles, Expats and Exotic Others by Robert Friedman
The Winter Spider by Doc Krinberg

Coming Soon:
The Princess in My Head by J. G. Matheny

Aignos Publishing | an imprint of Savant Books and Publications
http://www.aignospublishing.com

Made in the USA
Columbia, SC
29 June 2021